The Yeshua Sanction

ISBN: 0-6155-5152-1
ISBN-13: 9780615551524

The Yeshua Sanction

Book Two:
The Mikveh Scrolls

Steven G. Lightfoot

Dedication

This second book in *The Mikveh Scrolls* series represents a journey of discovery. It represents a calling to fulfill that command, given to us by Our Lord Jesus Christ in the *Book of Matthew,* which we know as The Great Commission.

Such a calling is not entered into lightly, but with prayerful consideration, and with the support of a community of the faithful. As with book one, my most steadfast support has come from my family.

And, this endeavor could not have made its way to the printed page without the love and inspiration, given to me so selflessly and in such magnificent abundance, by my God-sent wife, Angela, and our amazing children.

Sweetest Angela...your faith, your grace, your wit and your beauty captivate me completely. You remain, always, my *Angelica*.

Acknowledgement

I would like to formally thank my daughter, Brittany McReynolds, for her wonderful contributions to *The Yeshua Sanction* project. Not only did she pen the magnificent *Foreword,* which so eloquently captured the essence and purpose of this book; but, she also used her amazing, God-given artistic ability to create the powerful watercolor painting that serves beautifully as the cover art.

Brittany, you are without a doubt, a wonderful woman of faith. I can only imagine the tremendous ways that God will use you for His Glory during the course of your life. I thank God for the privilege of being your dad. May your Father in heaven bless you, your husband, Dane, and your future ministry, all the days of your lives.

Foreword
by Brittany McReynolds

My dad has always been a soldier to me. All that I know of him has been centered on that very aspect of his life. As a young girl I remember flipping through photo albums, put together by my grandparents, full of newspaper clippings and photographs of my dad during Desert Storm. I would marvel at the images: my dad and his fellow soldiers in full Marine combat gear next to the contents of an artillery transport vehicle they had intercepted, or a man coming out of a bunker holding his hands in surrender, or the fires across the horizon from the burning oil wells. I think he's always had a sense for adventure. He would write home to us, and we loved his letters; such amazing stories of life in a place my sisters and I could only imagine. Perhaps he made it more interesting and whimsical for our sakes, nothing out of the ordinary for a dad with three daughters.

After his time was up serving in the Marine Corps, life was an adjustment. After-all, once a Marine, always a Marine. He would wake in the middle of the night in a terror, reliving his experiences in the war. Until he found Christ I think he was at war with himself. What I know is that with Christ, he is not the man he once was. There is a peace within him that wasn't present before, like the battle within is finally over. Now he is a soldier for Christ. His motives have changed and where there once was a man who fought for personal glory, as we all have done; there is now a man who is fighting a very real spiritual battle for the Kingdom of God.

In his previous book, _The Mikveh Scrolls_, he brings to light the reality of this spiritual battle that we are all a part of. He shows us how God's plan is bigger than our own and while we may not know the outcome, we can trust that He has it under control, and in that we find peace. When all around there is chaos and turmoil, we take refuge in the knowledge that Jesus has risen and sits on the throne. This is our hope. It is what lifts us up from the depths, and carries us into new life with Christ.

If I have learned anything about a Christ-life it is this: that it is a life of complete surrender, of total unselfishness, wholly open to the guiding of the Holy Spirit and the will of God. Simply put, it's not about me. When we closely examine the character of God, we see a God who is all about His people. _"I am the Lord your God,"_ He says, _"who brought you out of the land of Egypt, out of the house of slavery. You shall have no other gods before me...for I the Lord your God am a jealous God."_ (Exodus 20:1-3, 5) In the Old Testament we see a God who is jealous for His people, who is angry over injustice to the thing He loves most. Why do we have anger? We have anger because we have love. God's wrath in the Old Testament is a direct result of the love for His creation. He is jealous for His bride. He longs, He aches for her affection and patiently waits for her to turn back to Him. The New Testament, the gospel of Christ, is our Lord's solution to the problem of a rebellious people who continue to choose self over their Creator, and who do not have the means to pay the debt of sin that they owe.

Love is an essential part of the character of God. God is love. All that He does stems from this aspect of His Being; He is incapable of doing anything less than that which is the highest good for His creation. That is the essence of love. It is a choice to put others before myself, to count their needs as above my own, namely that they have right relationship with the Father for that is the highest good for all people. Our responsibilities as Christians are simple: know Him, and make Him known. We are all in a spiritual battle, realized or not. If we live for Christ, we are called to extend the kingdom, for to live for Christ is to live as He lived, to be conformed to His image by the inner work of the Holy Spirit, and to give no less than He gave—everything.

Yet it is important to remember that God will never call us to something without providing the means to carry out the task. We often find ourselves thinking we must make some radical change in our life, or we have to meet "this" standard, or be at "this" point in our lives before God can use us. All it takes is a single step. "Use me God. I'm not much, but if you can turn water to wine, you can transform me to do wonders for your Kingdom." All He needs is a willing heart. He does not call the equipped, He equips the called. Jesus called his disciples not because they were men of renown known for Godly character and charitable nature. They were fishermen and tax collectors. But they believed, and they gave everything they had to follow Him. He called, they responded, He revealed.

Before the ascension, Jesus spoke his final words to the eleven disciples. *"All authority in heaven and on earth has been given to me. Go therefore and make disciples of all nations, baptizing them in the name of the Father and of the Son and of the Holy Spirit, teaching them to observe all that I have commanded you. And behold, I am with you always, to the end of the age."* (Matthew 28:18-20) This was the final command given to the disciples; moreover, the mandate given to all believers. *"Go therefore and make disciples of all nations."* I believe 2 Timothy 2:2 says it best, *"and what you have heard from me in the presence of many witnesses entrust to faithful men who will be able to teach others also."* Disciples, making disciples, making disciples: teaching others how to walk with God, and sending them out to do the same.

And we do not go out alone. *"And behold, I am with you always, to the end of the age."* In the book of Joshua, I am reminded of a very important fact: that Jesus will always go before us. Before the Israelites crossed the Jordan the Lord commanded that the priests bear the Ark of the Covenant, and pass before the people of Israel into the Jordan that they all might cross.

At the end of the three days the officers went through the camp and commanded the people, 'As soon as you see the ark of the covenant of the Lord your God being carried by the Levitical priests, then you shall set out from your place and follow it. Yet there shall be a distance between you and it, about 2,000 cubits in length. Do not come near it, in order that you may know the way you shall go, for you have not passed this way before.' Then Joshua said to the people, 'Consecrate yourselves, for tomorrow the Lord will do wonders among you.' And Joshua said to the priests, 'Take up the ark of the covenant and pass on before the people.' So they took up the ark of the covenant and went before the people. (Joshua 3:2-6).

We do not always know the way that we should go, but God goes before us. He cultivates the soil and prepares the way for us before we even begin the journey. My husband Dane and I struggled with our call to the mission field at first. Admittedly I struggled more so than he, being afraid of such a weighty calling and what it would mean for our lives. I was afraid of the uncertainty of things, and of the sacrifices we may have to make. What would it mean for our plans for a family? What dangers would we face? Will I be able to communicate back home with my family and how will I be able to live without having them so close? All of the fears were quieted by the knowledge that the Lord knows all these things. He knows our fears, and He knows the sacrifice He is asking us to make. Jesus relates to every fear, and every sacrifice. But the fact of the matter is the eternal consequence far outweighs the sacrifice...every time. Jesus willingly drank the cup given him knowing that the weight of eternity was greater than the weight of suffering. Love, after all, won out. There's a song by Justin Rizzo that states, "This momentary light affliction is working in me an eternal weight of glory." When we set our eyes upon the Lord the things we suffer are as nothing compared to the glory being stored in heaven.

God calls us to things we don't always find ourselves prepared for, and perhaps we feel unqualified to carry out the task. The beautiful thing about the Lord is that He trusts us enough to give us responsibility even when we think we are unqualified. In giving us responsibility He restores dignity to His people, and uses us to build His kingdom. The Great Commission is the calling, and the privilege we are given to carry out the work of Christ on earth, that all might hear and have the opportunity for relationship with Jesus.

The night the Lord confirmed our call to the mission field, to the unreached, I was overwhelmed by the Spirit of God. Dane and I had been wrestling with so many things. The week we arrived back from our honeymoon, reality hit in a big way, and the Lord started working something major in us. We had a restlessness on our hearts and after some time were certain the Lord was stirring something up within us. So, back to that night, sitting on the floor in the front of the church during worship, seeking answers desperately from the Lord, needing to know what He wanted from us, He answered. All I could do was weep. There was a breaking in my soul and the relief I felt in my innermost being flooded me with emotion and I wept, I sang praises to God because there was no more confusion, no more wrestling, just clarity and peace...*such* peace. Our calling was so clear.

In that moment, resting within the presence of God, nothing seemed impossible, nothing seemed too daunting; all I had to offer was freely given for His purpose because of my love for Him, and when I remember that, I rejoice. God will always go before us, He will always equip those He calls, and when we give our lives wholly to Him, He will truly do immeasurably more than we can imagine. But we must respond, and we must go, for with knowledge comes responsibility, and our work is not finished.

But how are they to call on him in whom they have not believed? And how are they to believe in him of whom they have never heard? And how are they to hear without someone preaching? And how are they to preach unless they are sent? As it is written, "How beautiful are the feet of those who preach the good news!" (Romans 10:14-15).

Author's Note

If you read the first book in this series, _The Mikveh Scrolls_, and then read the magnificent _Foreword_ by Brittany McReynolds, which opens this book, then you are by now aware that the focus of this series is The Great Commission of Our Lord and Savior Jesus Christ. The very title of this book speaks volumes about its content: _Yeshua_, Aramaic for Jesus; _Sanction_, meaning _mandate_ or _commission_. Indeed, not only is it the underlying theme of the content of these books, but it is their very purpose as well. For it is my sincere hope that my words will inspire those who are seeking, to look deeper into the possibility of a very real, very personal relationship with the Living Christ. I recommend that all seekers explore the source of God's Word as contained in the pages of _The Bible,_ and look to the community of faith for guidance and teaching to help build your new faith and keep you on the right path.

No doubt some of you reading this are already on that path. If so, welcome brother or sister, and please enjoy the adventure. And, when you have finished reading, please share this book with someone you know who could use the Truth in their life, so that they too may know Christ.

I want to take a moment and warn those who have read the first book; that _The Yeshua Sanction_ deals very directly with the powers and principalities mentioned in the eighth chapter of *Romans*. This book is quite a bit darker than the first. The use of demons and the person of Satan represent the very worst of the opposition in the spiritual battle in which each of us is engaged. Make no mistake; though the book is fiction, the battle is real. And, here is where the warning must be issued: In the reality of most of the lives of the unsaved, the battle is often lost, not because of direct confrontation with the forces of darkness, represented by horned creatures of Dante-like imagery, but rather because of the deceiver's divisive use of our own apathy, and the very nature of fallen man to act sinfully, which drives a wedge between humankind and God. And, if by their intentional diversions, the demons can distract us long enough so that we miss the opportunities for salvation along the road of life, until we ultimately reach its end, then they win, one poor misguided soul at a time.

As I read my daughter, Brittany's, beautiful *Foreword*, I am both humbled and honored. I am humbled that God has chosen to use me as an instrument to spread the good news of Jesus Christ and his mission to save us from sure and eternal separation from God, which we wholly deserve. I am humbled that He loved us so much that He would sacrifice His only son as payment for our sins.

I am honored that my daughter regards me as a soldier for the Kingdom. I can think of no greater purpose for my life. I am honored that she recognizes the change in me because of the saving grace of God as poured out to me through Jesus Christ. And, I am honored that God granted me a daughter so maturely grounded in her faith and so committed to a life of service to Him alongside her husband, Dane. Truly, I am so very blessed by all of my children.

Finally, as my wife, Angela, and I discussed Brittany's words; about how they had inspired both of us to the point of tears; and, about how perfectly they had set the tone for this book; Angela, who is an inspired woman of faith in her own right, made this astute observation:

"The statement Brittany wrote, which keeps playing over and over in my mind is *'God doesn't call the equipped, He equips the called.'* What a profound statement of truth that is. As Christians, we too often dismiss what God is calling us to do because we think we are not educated enough or bold enough or *equipped* enough to carry out His mission. But in reality, that is the essence of our Faith: Hearing the calling and casting aside those doubts in OUR abilities and trusting in HIS, because He is the *Great I Am*. He is all things. Things we hope for, things we trust in, things we need. I think it is the fear of not being able to hold up our end of the bargain that prevents us from completely opening up to His call. Faith and trust in Him will never leave us doubting whether or not we have the ability to fulfill His calling, once we hear it."

To Angela's observation I can only add a very heartfelt, *Amen.*

Oh, and one last thought: All characters appearing in this work are fictitious. Any resemblance to real persons, living or dead, is purely coincidental. That being said, if you feel that you resemble one of the characters in this book who is of questionable, er...character, then I have but one word of advice for you; *repent!* There is a high probability that you need Jesus.

chapter

ONE

Then the fifth angel sounded, and I saw a star from heaven which had fallen to the earth; and the key to the bottomless pit was given to him.

He opened the bottomless pit, and smoke went up out of the pit, like the smoke of a great furnace; and the sun and the air were darkened by the smoke of the pit.

—Revelation 9:1-2

KUWAIT. AL-BURQAN OIL FIELDS. FEBRUARY 1991.

A rushing wind. That's what it sounded like. An unceasing, deafening, violently rushing wind. First Lieutenant

Geoffrey Proudman, USMC, shoved grimy, yellow, foam earplugs into his ears in an attempt to muffle the noise. He tried in vain to wipe the oily mist from his goggles, but only succeeded in smearing the dark brown droplets around the lenses. The thin scarf covering his nose and mouth was saturated with oil, as were his clothes and hair. "Will I ever be clean again?" he thought. He could taste the oil. He could smell the oil. All of his senses were smothered in it. Opening the door to his Hummer, Proudman motioned to Corporal Klark for the radio handset. Klark obliged. Proudman removed the earplug from his right ear, depressed the key twice, listening for the familiar break in static before he spoke, "Alpha One, Alpha One, this is Lima One Alpha, over."

"Lima One Alpha, this is Alpha One, go ahead, over."

"Alpha One, prepare to copy Bravo Delta Alpha [Battle Damage Assessment] for last fire mission, over."

"Roger, Lima One Alpha, send your BDA, over."

"BDA: Target destroyed. Estimate two zero enemy KIA, over."

"Roger, Lima One Alpha, I copy, target destroyed, two zero enemy KIA, over."

"Correct copy, Alpha One. Nice shooting. Lima One Alpha, out."

Proudman tossed the handset back to Klark and said, "Wait one." He closed the Hummer door, replaced the earplug into his ear, and walked cautiously up the draw toward the smoldering bunker upon which he had just called artillery fire. Fifty meters to his right was the source of the constant din: a burning oil well set ablaze by the Iraqi forces as they fell back from Kuwait. The burning oil gushed from its mouth with the ear-splitting rush of a jet engine. Along the horizon, the landscape was dotted with a hundred more just like it. The noonday sky was black as night and the constant oil rain coated everything. If there were ever hell on earth, this was it.

Proudman approached the bunker slowly, his M16A2 service rifle at the ready. He could feel the oily sweat running down his back. His neck hair bristled and he felt oddly chilled despite the heat radiating off of the smoldering bunker and the adjacent oil well's inferno. The earplugs in his ears made him overly aware of the sounds coming from his own body. His neck creaked and popped as he bobbled his head from sided to side, wishing the stiffness would work itself out. He pushed a wooden beam away from the bunker's opening with his foot and crouched to peer inside over the top of his rifle sights. His finger applied the slightest pressure to the M16's trigger, and his thumb clicked the rifle's selector lever from single-shot to three-round-burst, ready to unload on the slightest movement if necessary. The unmistakable stench of burning flesh hit him squarely in the face and he recoiled from it. Re-adjusting his scarf over his nose, he again peered into the opening, this time prepared for the oppressive atmosphere. He lifted the goggles off of his face and up onto his forehead. Instantly he could see more clearly the carnage that was strewn about the bunker. "Efficient," he thought. "Devastatingly efficient." The artillery shells had burst in the air above the bunker and dispersed hundreds of shape-charges, which upon impact, blew perfect holes in the bunker's roof and spewed molten shrapnel throughout its interior, shredding anything inside.

Stepping down into the bunker, Proudman reached for his Maglite. He removed the red lens and let the white light illuminate the bunker's interior. He saw that the bunker was an old cargo container that had been too shallowly buried in the desert sand. The faces of the dead, those that still had faces, looked blankly back at him. Proudman felt watched. He tried to ignore the feeling as he poked through the rubble for anything usable, either by him, by S-2 or by the enemy. He noticed a field radio partially covered by an Iraqi body. Proudman rolled the body off of the radio and made a note of the frequency to which it was set. "Might need that intel," he said to himself.

His estimate of twenty dead was fairly accurate, although, for the life of him, he couldn't tell whose limbs belonged to whom and how many bodies were actually there. Seeing nothing else of interest, Proudman backed his way to the mouth of the bunker. As he carefully avoided stepping on anything moist, he shuddered at the thought of having to clean anything from the tread of his boot. Pulling himself out of the bunker, he jerked a thermite grenade from his web-gear and removed the pin. Releasing the spoon from his grip, he watched as it sprung a short distance into the sand. He held the triggered grenade for longer than he knew he should before tossing it into the bunker. He then walked purposefully back toward the Hummer as the grenade completed the artillery's devastation.

"Nice." Corporal Klark offered as Proudman climbed into the Hummer.

"Yeah...nice," Proudman muttered. "Let's clear this grid. Don't want to be around for any counter-fire."

Klark gunned the motor and the Hummer jolted, spinning its wheels in the oily sand. Proudman could still see the hollow eyes of the dead looking after them as they drove away. Those eyes would haunt his mind for the rest of his days and mercilessly torment his restless nights. This hell would surely follow him.

ISRAEL. PRESENT DAY.

The Reverend Geoffrey Proudman stirred from a restless sleep. The hollow-eyed faces of his nightmares faded from his mind's eye. He opened his eyes slightly and saw the lightening sky through a gap in the tent flap. He guessed that the time was about 6:00 in the morning. The desert air was cool and crisp and a slight breeze moved across his face. It had been six weeks since *The Gathering* at Herodium and the revelation of *The Mikveh Scrolls*.

Since then, Proudman had been moving through the camps of the gathered, teaching the new Christians the basic tenets of their new faith, answering questions and encouraging them as they prepared to make their way back to their homes. In fact many had already dispersed and those that were left were merely waiting out the shortages of air transportation out of Israel. Proudman estimated that the remnant numbered less than ten thousand now. In another week, they too would be gone and Proudman would be in search of transportation back to the United States shortly thereafter. His time here in Israel was coming to an end.

Proudman knew he had loose ends to tie, not the least of which was Simon Cross' marriage to Rachel Rosenkranz. He had promised them that he would perform the ceremony before he left the dig at Herodium to begin carrying out the Great Commission commanded at *The Gathering*. He smiled at the thought of the two of them becoming husband and wife. They deserved each other. Both were committed Christians. Both were archaeologists. Both were hopelessly in love...with their Lord and with one another. In a relatively short time, they had become his dearest friends. Partly so, Proudman knew, because of all they had experienced together as they moved obediently in God's will to discover *The Mikveh Scrolls*. What an adventure they had lived! How wonderful to witness God moving powerfully in the midst of His people!

Proudman sat up on his cot and wiped the sleep from his eyes. He rubbed his hand over his stubbly face and chin. He needed a shave. He wanted a shower. His hygiene for the past six weeks had been limited to bathing and shaving from his canteen cup, a skill he had perfected in the deserts of Kuwait and Iraq during the war. He sat day dreaming of a hot, flowing shower with soap and shampoo; a slice of heaven.

"Father Proudman?" A young girl's voice called softly from outside his tent flap. "Father Proudman, are you up?" It was Victoria, the youngest member of the family camped nearby. Proudman had spent the last few days teaching her family, and others in the area, about their new faith. Victoria's family...some of her family, anyway, had responded to the call of *The Gathering* and had travelled from Houston, Texas. And, like so many others, leaving their homes, dropping everything to sit at the base of Mt. Herod and receive whatever God had to give them. They had no idea what they were in for. They only knew that they had to make the journey, as if some unseen force within their very core was driving them to Herodium.

"Yes, Missy, I'm up." Proudman used Victoria's nickname. In the short time he had known her, she had become like family. She was just 14 and the tiniest of things. Her dirty-blonde hair was a little longer than shoulder length, and straight. She had bright eyes and an impish smile, as if she were always up to something. She was never shy, from the moment Proudman had walked into their encampment; Missy had taken to him like a shadow. She was hungry for her new faith. She would sit for hours listening to Proudman telling the people about Jesus. When Proudman would ask, "Are there any questions?" Missy's hand was always first to rocket into the air, and a thoughtful, intelligent question would follow. Proudman knew she would be the rock of faith in her family.

"I brought you some biscuits and jam." Missy peered through the opening in the tent flap. "We had extra."

"Well now, that's mighty generous of you Miss Priss! Thanks!"

"You're welcome. Can I come in?"

"Of course, but tie that tent flap back for me on your way in so we can make the most of the breeze while we have it."

"K. Here." Missy handed Proudman the plate of biscuits and jam and turned to tie up the tent flap. "We're heading to the airport today."

"Yes, I know."

"Do you think I'm ready to be a Christian on my own, Father Proudman? I mean...it's only been a few days."

"Well, ya see, Missy...that's the really great thing about being a Christian...you never have to do it on your own! Your family and friends will be there to help you and keep you accountable. You'll join a good church when you get back home, and your whole community of faith will help you stay on the path you have so wisely chosen."

"But my family and friends are all new Christians too. And, nobody in my family has ever really been to a church other than at Christmas and Easter...How will we do this without you there to answer our questions and to make sure we're doing it right!?"

Proudman laughed. "OMG, Missy!" Proudman tried to sound as much like a teenage girl as he could muster. "You and I will totally be bff's, like totally, K?"

Missy laughed the delightful chuckle that Proudman had grown so fond of.

"Listen, seriously, Victoria. You've got this. Your faith will grow and you will be an amazing young woman of faith. Church is not hard. You'll find people there who will laugh with you, cry with you, share their faith with you... and rejoice in your faith as well. You'll see. Trust me on this. More importantly...trust Him on this." Proudman pointed skyward.

"Okay." Missy nodded slowly. "But I'll miss you. Is that ok, Father Proudman?...if I miss you?"

"Of course it is. I will miss you too, Victoria."

"Missy. My best friends call me Missy."

"I will miss you too, Missy." Proudman smiled.

Missy smiled back and slipped out of the tent as softly as she had arrived.

Proudman sat looking after her. What an impression she had made on him. "Lord," Proudman prayed. "Bless that child with a long and happy life. Wrap her in your loving, protective arms and keep her safe. Grant her your grace, your wisdom, your mercy and your steadfast loving kindness all the days of her life. In Jesus' name. Amen."

HELL. PRESENT DAY.

"Bring me that idiot, Abbas!" seethed Abaddon.

"Yes, my lord," hissed the demon Baal. "I will have him brought before you immediately. I have taken the liberty of personally torturing him since his untimely arrival in the abyss."

"Your most insidious torment is nothing compared to the agony I have in store for him. Mahmoud Abbas... bumbling fool." Abaddon spat the name out as if it were something putrid on his tongue. "I gave him power over my armies on Earth and bid him simply eradicate those God-worshipping Jews...How hard a task was that? And what do I get for my loving kindness and generosity? Failure! My armies destroyed! A new fervor for Christ! *The Gathering*! Those damn scrolls! Maddening!"

Baal cringed at Abaddon's every rant. As powerful as Baal was in Hell, his power was small compared to Abaddon. Known by many names, Abaddon ruled Hell with intimidation and fear. He was Lucifer, Apollyon...Satan. Baal hastened out of Abaddon's presence to see what was keeping Mahmoud Abbas. Better to quickly give Abaddon someone else to vent his wrath upon.

Mahmoud Abbas, ordained by Abaddon as leader of the Islamic Alliance, had done what no other man had been able to accomplish. He had united the Sunnis and Shiites under one flag. Using the Palestinian / Israeli conflict, he had rallied Islamic fundamentalist forces into a massive army, which he wasted no time unleashing against Israel. If it had not been for the intervention of Almighty God, using Proudman, Simon Cross and his team as instruments during the battle at the Dome of the Rock, Abbas would have crushed Israel forever. But God was mighty that day, and Proudman and his friends were strong in their faith. Abbas crumbled like sand, along with his army. The Dome of the Rock was reduced to rubble, shaken off of the Holy Temple Mount like so much dust.

It was this defeat and his resulting death that delivered Abbas into the abyss. It was this failure that angered Abaddon so. Mahmoud Abbas was about to reap the reward of his sacrifice to Allah, and it was not seventy-two virgins in paradise. Far from it!

Abaddon paced impatiently. His anger raged deep within him, causing deep blue veins in his neck and on his forehead to pop in sharp contrast to his pale white skin.

His normally beautiful countenance morphed into a contorted representation of the vileness of his soulless existence. His enormous pride bruised and broken, hatred and rage rushed in to fill the void. He imagined the endless torment he would release upon Abbas. Would he strip the flesh from his bones? Would he snap his neck, heal it and snap it again, over and over until the end of time? Would he have the hounds of Hell devour him? The possibilities for torture and eternal anguish were endless...How would he repay Abbas for his incompetence?

Baal reappeared with Abbas in his clawed grasp. He tossed Abbas at Abaddon's feet as if he were throwing scraps to the dogs. Abbas landed in a whimpering heap, crying, "Allah, save me."

"Allah, save me," Abaddon mocked. "Do you think that some insignificant, made-up moon god has any power to remove you from my grasp? Go ahead, you sniveling coward...call to Allah. Call him. Call him. CALL HIM!! Here we'll do it together." Abaddon began to chant, "Allah, save me. Allah, save me. Allah, save me. WHY ARE YOU NOT CALLING HIM!!!?" Abaddon choked Abbas' neck as he spewed hatred into his face. "Allah, save me. ALLAH, SAVE ME!!!" The Destroyer pulled his hand away from Abbas' throat, drawing blood with his fingernails as he did so.

Abbas squealed helplessly. He resumed whimpering, no longer invoking the name of his powerless pagan deity.

"You've failed me," Abaddon said softly. The softness of his tone was more unsettling to Abbas than his booming, maniacal yell. "I gave you power and your heart's desire, and you failed me. You believe that your precious Allah will reward you with seventy-two virgins in paradise, am I correct? So, since Allah, like you, failed to deliver...I, Satan, will provide you with your reward. Baal, see if we can find seventy-two poxed hell hounds to ravage our friend Mahmoud. How would you like that Abbas? I hear crazed hell hounds are quite voracious in their appetites. And just so your reward is not over too quickly, we will slow down time so that you can watch their dripping fangs rip you apart for the next thousand years. How does that sound, hmm?"

"Mercy, please," Abbas moaned.

"BE GONE! BAAL, FEED THIS MEAT TO THE HOUNDS!"

Baal skewered Abbas' thigh with his clawed grip and dragged the squealing, pleading mess out of Abaddon's sight. Abaddon smiled with self-satisfaction. The hell hounds would eat well, and slowly, for the next thousand years.

"Baal! After you dispose of the trash, return to me so we can discuss this...*Gathering*!" Abaddon hissed as he spoke the words. The very thought of humans worshipping God filled him with seething jealousy and rage. He would not stand for it! His mind searched through the blackness for an outlet for his vengeance. He wasn't sure how, but he would not rest until the souls of those responsible were shrieking in torment. The need for their destruction consumed him. Nothing else mattered.

chapter

TWO

You therefore, my son, be strong in the grace that is in Christ Jesus.

The things which you have heard from me in the presence of many witnesses, entrust these to faithful men who will be able to teach others also.

- 2 Timothy 2:1-2

Geoffrey Proudman devoured the last homemade biscuit Victoria had given him. It was delightfully smoky from baking in the coals of a campfire. The strawberry jam's sweetness played well on his palette with the smokiness. "Delicious," he said to himself, wiping his hands on his grubby jeans.

Stretching as he rose from his cot, Proudman moved to the tent's opening and looked out at the remnant of *The Gathering*. Camps dotted the landscape around Mt. Herod and around the ruins of Lower Herodium. Everywhere there were seekers preparing a morning meal or packing up for the trip into Jerusalem, and then home. Next to his tent was the still smoldering fire pit from Victoria's family's campsite. They had just departed, leaving Proudman feeling empty and alone. But, there was much work yet to be accomplished and no time to wallow in the feeling.

The Reverend Proudman picked up his backpack. In it were his *Bible*, excessively worn from much use in the field the past few weeks, his *Book of Common Prayer*, which was equally tattered, a silver tube of communion wafers, a flask of wine, an alabaster vile of anointing oil with an ornate silver stopper, a small (but substantial) alter cross, and a silver flask of holy water, engraved with a cross. Hoisting the pack over one shoulder, Proudman grasped a gnarled walking stick he had fashioned from an olive branch. He didn't particularly need the stick to negotiate the rugged terrain, but it felt good in his hand and he liked it.

Missing from his backpack were the obvious necessities one might expect to pack for a day (or two) away from base camp, not the least of which were food and water. But, Proudman didn't give those things so much as a fleeting thought. For the many days he had spent in the field, teaching and preaching to the people since *The Gathering*, he had never gone hungry or thirsty. Everywhere he stopped, the seekers would always offer him some of their provisions. Countless times he had shared a meal with strangers who fast became friends over broken bread. Like manna from heaven, God always provided for his sustenance.

Setting out on his day's journey, Proudman decided to hike toward Lower Herodium. He had made the trek to the outer camps for many weeks now, so he thought he would concentrate his efforts on the camps that remained closer in to the base of Mt. Herod. Only a few more days of this and all the people will have gone. It was strange to him that his mission in Israel was drawing to a close. So many lives had been touched by his gospel message. He couldn't possibly count them all. And, he couldn't possibly know how many had been saved during and immediately after the events at *The Gathering*, but he knew it was many. "Praise God," he thought.

As he walked, Proudman began to think of Simon and Rachel. His proximity to Lower Herodium made it entirely possible that he might pay them a visit at the dig. How good it would be to see them again. Perhaps they would be ready for him to marry them! What a joyous occasion that would be! Proudman suddenly realized that all seemed right with the world. How could it not be? Israel had been spared from destruction at the hands of Mahmoud Abbas and the armies of the Islamic Alliance, *The Gathering* had brought thousands upon thousands to know Christ in an instant of spiritual revelation, the world was in a state of holy transformation from the secular to the divine, and Proudman was fulfilling his calling in the spirit of The Great Commission commanded by Christ in the *Book of Matthew*. What could possibly make it any better except Jesus Christ returning now?

Proudman approached a cluster of tents set on the edge of an ancient pool, once used by members of Herod's court. What an oasis it must have been in Herod's day, with cool water providing relief from the arid environment. The square pool was lined with hewn stone, and there was a round structure in the center, like an island, made of the same stone blocks. On the Mt. Herod side, there was a row of broken columns, a mere echo of their former greatness. Still, even in ruins, Proudman could sense the grandeur that once existed here. He could imagine people enjoying the water's coolness, with Herod's manmade conical mountain providing the backdrop.

As the reverend entered the center of the tents, a group of seekers was just finishing breakfast. "Hello," Proudman offered.

"Hello," the group said, almost as if they were one voice.

Proudman assessed there were about thirty people, men and women, teenagers, and children. There was a banner spanning a white, portable canopy on which was printed, *Radiant United Methodist Church, Humble, Texas.* "Outstanding," he thought, "a missionary group from the

States!" It was a good feeling to realize that others were taking it upon themselves to bring the new Christians of *The Gathering* along in their faith quest.

"My name is Geoffrey Proudman. I'm a priest. Episcopal."

"Welcome." The response was enthusiastic. "We're a mission team from Texas. We call ourselves Methodists, but most of us were something else...or nothing else, before we formed *Radiant*...that's the name of our church, you see. Our mission is to radiate the light of Christ."

"It's really good to see you. I hadn't realized that you were working in the area. I've been traveling among the outer camps, preaching and teaching since *The Gathering*."

"You're not just a priest," one of the group spoke up, "You're THE priest! I recognize your voice!"

"My voice, but God's words," Proudman offered humbly.

"Of course, but still an honor. Can we offer you some breakfast? There's plenty left and it won't keep."

"No thank you. I've had breakfast, but if you have some water, I'd be grateful."

"Yes, of course." One of the teenage girls retrieved a bottle of water from a cooler and, smiling, brought it to Geoffrey. "It's not all that cold. No ice," she said shyly.

"But it's cool and wet, young lady, and that's good enough. Thank you...really."

The girl danced away from Proudman. How full of joy and life she seemed as she laughed and giggled with another girl in the group. Proudman watched as the two interacted, spinning in unison as if they were practicing a dance routine. "High school dance team?" Proudman asked no one in particular.

"Yes. My daughter and her friend," one of the ladies in the group raised her hand. "They never stop spinning!"

"I can see that." Proudman was elated at having come upon this group of missionaries. He decided to spend some time here. It would be good to get <u>his</u> spiritual batteries charged for a change.

"Please, Padre, come and sit for a while. Tell us about your travels!"

Proudman nodded and moved to a canvas chair, dropping his pack to the ground. He placed his water bottle in the mesh drink holder stitched into the chair's arm and placed his walking stick across his pack. As he did so, he looked around the group at each face. They all smiled back at him. "I'm Matt," one said.

"Michelle, I'm Matt's wife," said another.

"Cris, here!" the dancer's mom chimed in.

"Bre," said the dancer from somewhere within a spin.

"Allie," called out the dancer's twirling friend.

One by one each person introduced themselves. "Nice to meet all of you. Is that everyone?" Geoffrey asked.

"I think so...wait, where's Angie?" Cris asked. "I don't think she even ate breakfast this morning. She must still be in the tent."

From behind Proudman, a sweet voice called, "Here I am!"

All at once, Proudman's senses began to tingle. "That voice!" he thought. "I know that voice!" He could almost feel the deep recognition rising in his core. His heart skipped a beat as the realization crept in. The voice echoed in his memory...no, wait...it wasn't memory; it was from a more distant place. Deeper than memory. More profound. It was from his subconscious mind...a dream. Yes! But which dream? His mind raced. Not just one dream, but many dreams...a lifetime of dreams.

His thoughts began to fall into place, and the voice recalled a familiar image. How many times the image had appeared in his dreams, he couldn't possibly count. His mind reeled as he recalled the countless times he had sat, knees to the earth, praying for God to answer this specific prayer. He had told no one about her permeating his dreams, his thoughts, his heart, until the day he shared his faith story with Simon and Rachel, Jordan and Miriam, and Moishe, when they first set out for Herodium a lifetime ago. They had thought it both wonderful and sad that he was in love with a woman he had only seen in his dreams. But he was sure that the dreams were God's way of telling him to wait patiently for the one woman who God had planned for him. The dreams were so very tangible, as if she were flesh and blood. Her features were always the same, never varied. And she had told him her name. The very name that now came rushing from deep within his core, through the center of his heart, into his brain.

As the voice reverberated in his ears, her image began to materialize in his head. Long, sometimes straight, sometimes wavy, always silky, brunette hair. Slate-blue, soul-piercing eyes. Inviting smile, which could easily become a mischievous grin. Proudman couldn't believe it. "Angelica," he said out loud. The name burst from his lips as a statement of fact, not a question.

"Yes," answered the voice behind him. "Do I know you? I mean, have we met before?"

Proudman spun in his chair and nearly fell over in the process. His eyes confirmed what his mind had envisioned. It was her! The one he'd prayed for all those years. Right down to the last detail, she was his Angelica! Proudman tried to remain composed. "No, we haven't met exactly...," he watched as Angelica pulled her hair into a ponytail. His mouth dropped open a bit and he bit his lower lip as he took in the curve of her body while she wrapped a band around her hair. He wondered if anybody could tell he had noticed her in that way, but at the same time he didn't really care what anyone thought. She was beautiful and he was not only a priest...he was, after all, a man. "Way to go, God!" he thought.

"So if we haven't exactly met, then how do you know me? I mean you said my name as if you knew me...didn't you?" Angelica was confused. While in her mind she knew she had never met the priest, in her heart she felt an instant connection. She sensed she knew him. She decided that to just sit next to him and see what happened next was the best course of action. She sat, looked at Geoffrey and smiled.

Geoffrey Proudman's senses were instantly over-whelmed. The breeze Angelica created when she moved into the chair next to him was heavenly-scented. Her po-nytail brushed his cheek when she quickly turned her head, and its silkiness and fragrance made him warm inside. As she sat, her incredibly long legs crossed in front of her, and Proudman sat speechless, entranced by the way her foot, with its delicately painted toes, bounced rhythmically at the end of her shapely leg, while precariously dangling a flip-flop. Proudman was attracted to her, no question. It was not a lustful attraction by any means, but the healthy interest, make that desire, of a man for a woman as designed by the Creator.

"So, Reverend...tell us of your time here at *The Gathering*," one of the group spoke up; breaking Proudman's trance and bringing him back to earth.

Abaddon sat stewing in his rage. "If you want something done diabolically well, then you have to do it yourself," he seethed. "Humans, at least the one's not spoken for, are so easily influenced to do one's bidding," he reasoned to himself. "The problem is that they are so weak and unreliable. Yes, they are incapable of saving themselves regardless, so their souls are easily acquired, but getting them to effectively carry out one's plans is quite another matter... they're just so...frail and incompetent." He rose from his chair and paced. He felt as if he were on the verge of something...a solution to this recent irritant in Israel. The name of a place was haunting his mind. "What is that place?" he thought. "What is that name? What evil took place there, so dark that the very ground is cursed forever. Forever uninhabitable. Forever unholy." As he pondered, two demons appeared, one carrying a large ornate bowl and the other an enormous, equally gaudy cup. The demons scurried about readying their master's table. Plates, silver utensils with bone handles, and carafes of sour wine were placed appropriately.

Suddenly ravenous, Abaddon swatted a demon out of his way as he reached for the sharp, two-pronged fork next to the bowl. He breathed in over the bowl and salivated as his nostrils filled with the smell of roasted human and animal hearts, his favorite meal by far. "Excellent!" he drooled. The battered demon, undaunted, scurried back to the table and poured wine from two carafes into the large goblet. Abaddon skewered one of the hearts with the fork and stuffed it in his mouth, smacking his lips noisily; bits of chewed heart dropping from his open mouth. Before swallowing the mouthful, he snatched up the goblet and lifted it to drink, spilling foul wine over the cup's rim, down his chin and onto the table and floor. A gulp of wine washed the meat down his throat as he skewered another heart. He liked the richness of the animal hearts, but the more delicate flavor of the human hearts was just as appetizing to him. The disgusting feast continued until Abaddon had gorged himself into a gluttonous stupor.

Pushing away from the table, Abaddon staggered off to sleep, leaving the pair of demons to fight like crazed cats over the leftover scraps of chewed heart and puddles of spilt vinegar.

chapter

THREE

Now this man acquired a field with the price of his wickedness, and falling headlong, he burst open in the middle and all his intestines gushed out.

And it became known to all who were living in Jerusalem; so that in their own language that field was called Hakeldama, that is, Field of Blood.

"For it is written in the book of Psalms, 'LET HIS HOME-STEAD BE MADE DESOLATE, AND LET NO ONE DWELL IN IT'...

- Acts 1:18-20

Angelica Thorman was nothing less than an amazing woman of faith. Raised in the Catholic tradition, she had spent her childhood attending Catholic mass in the post chapel of army bases from Ft. Bragg, North Carolina to El Paso, Texas to Ansbach, Germany. She loved the liturgical church for its tradition and reverence, but as her thirst for a more personal relationship with Christ grew, she found herself less interested in the need for the intercessory services of a Catholic priest. Christ was, after all, <u>her</u> Lord and Savior, and she would approach His throne by His grace alone. She didn't require a priestly middleman.

Her faith journey was by no means a straight and narrow path. For with a Catholic upbringing, there is often a rebellious countermeasure, which for teenage Angelica proved to be much more enticing than the stuffiness of a confessional. Not that she was the proverbial bad girl either; her attention was just more drawn to the wonders of being a beautiful young woman in Europe, with a driver's license, a second hand BMW sedan, and plenty of young friends to fill all the seats. She was a girl in search of fun and freedom and bent on filling every hour of every day with exploring the old world in which she found herself thanks to her stepfather's career in the U.S. Army. Salvation was not the first thing on her mind.

When that career brought her family stateside again, Angelica again found herself in El Paso, Texas. Used to the freedom she enjoyed in Germany, and now a young woman come of age, she began working so that her freedom could continue. She was determined to live her life her way. While a girl of eighteen in Germany, she and her friends could legally drink in the local *Biergarten*. Now that she was home, and 21, she would continue to enjoy that freedom. It was at a local El Paso night spot where she met her husband. She was leaning against a wall, sipping a cocktail through a straw. "You're not out there getting your boogie on?" he said to her, loudly enough to be heard above the thumping dance music. Somehow those words led to marriage.

From that point, Angelica navigated the curved and hilly road of life. She was a working woman, a Navy wife and eventually a mom. In San Diego, she gave birth to her pride and joy, Alfredo. She called him Freddie and the very sight of him filled her heart. Life was busy, and therefore it seemed as if all was as it should be. As with most families, there were joys and sorrows, times of plenty and times of want. Church happened on occasion, especially Christmas and Easter. But there was no time, and perhaps little desire, to seek something deeper and more meaningful. Over time the marriage became strained and dissolved. Not so much from conflict perhaps, but more from lack of similar interests. Angelica wanted more of something; she just couldn't put her finger on what exactly. Her husband just wanted to maintain the status quo. But, she had a hole in her core being that nothing and nobody could fill. She would come to realize some years later that the hole was God-shaped.

Eventually, Angelica grew weary of the search to fill the hole in her soul. She needed rest, not so much physically as spiritually. It was then that she stepped for the first time into the small plant church tucked unobtrusively into a strip center in the shell of a former Food City grocery store. Angelica found salvation and peace in the Word as given each Sunday morning by a dynamic, evangelical preacher doing kingdom work disguised as a common Methodist pastor.

Geoffrey Proudman had just spent the last hour telling the *Radiant UMC* mission team about the events leading up to *The Gathering* and the discovery of the scrolls in the mikveh underneath Herodium. All present sat motionless, listening intently. Perhaps most intently, was Angelica, always hungry for more teaching to advance her in her faith journey. In this case, however, she was beginning to realize something more than the reverend's words. She was captivated by Proudman's commanding presence as a man of God, and she was beginning to be more interested in the man behind the collar. "What an interesting journey he's had, and what a rock-steady, unshakable faith," she thought as Proudman spoke to the group. "Certainly not the stuffy clergyman of my Catholic youth," Angelica mused.

Abaddon slept a tormented sleep. His countenance reverted to his more angelic appearance for brief periods between angry fits in his drunken slumber. As the rage surfaced, his physical appearance would morph from the angel of light into the beast of the abyss; an outward manifestation of the ugly evil within. As he slept, an image appeared in the darkness of his mind; a human form from within the nothingness of eternal separation from God. Drifting alone near the edge of the darkness, the figure teased Abaddon's memory. "Who are you and why do you haunt me so?" Abaddon muttered in unconsciousness. He could not make out the figure's face, but his form seemed familiar. He turned over in his sleep, agitated and restless. "Show yourself to me! What do you want?"

The figure, face in shadow, began to mouth a word; the name Abaddon had been trying to recall before the demons entered and prepared his table. The mouthing of the word became a low, labored moaning. Abaddon peered with his demonic eyes into the nothingness, into the shadow cloaking the figure's face. Gradually he began to see the distinctive features that defined this tormented soul. "Judas," he whispered in his sleep. "It is you! I gave you thirty pieces of silver for your trouble and you tossed them aside. And why? Out of guilt? Ridiculous! You are doubly damned...hated by men and cursed for eternity. What do you have to tell me pitiful one?"

Judas continued to mouth the word, his unseeing eyes staring past Abaddon as he felt nothing but separation, isolation and desperation. The word became more audible and intelligible. "Hakeldama," Judas groaned. "Hakeldama."

Abaddon knew that word. It was ancient. Almost forgotten. It was the dialect of the Jews; he knew it well. He despised it.

"Hakeldama! Hakeldama!" Judas continued more forcefully.

Abaddon searched his memory. Images of blood. Images of desolation. Thoughts of uninhabitable wilderness... a field where nothing could live; a field of blood. Abaddon jolted from sleep to consciousness. A wicked smile formed on his lips. Judas had given him the solution to *The Gathering* problem...Hakeldama! Abaddon was beside himself with anticipation.

Abaddon rose from his bed and crossed the room quickly to his massive desk. The desk was carved from an enormous tree stump. Gargoyles formed the feet, holding the desktop on their straining shoulders. Opening a large wooden drawer, he pulled out a hand-scribed *Bible*. He turned first to the *Book of Matthew* and read in Latin, the account of Judas, who after betraying Jesus, was overwhelmed with guilt and attempted to give back the thirty pieces of silver he had been paid for his betrayal. Abaddon read how the priests and elders did not want the money back, so Judas threw the money into the temple and hung himself from a tree, in a field, in the Valley of Hinnom, near Jerusalem.

Abaddon snickered as if reading a comic book. He turned quickly to the *Book of Acts*, and delighted in the text where it told of when Judas hung himself, fell and tore open his abdomen, and spilled his blood in the field. Abaddon cackled as he read the verses where, the priests could not put the blood money into the temple treasury, so they bought the field where Judas died and turned it into a cemetery for strangers and the poor. Abaddon was giddy as he read that the field was called Hakeldama, in Aramaic, which meant Field of Blood; so named because Judas' blood covered the ground and because the land was purchased with the price of blood—the blood of Jesus Christ.

Abaddon was immensely pleased. So cursed was the ground at Hakeldama that no dwelling had ever been built upon it. He knew that to this day, the only structure ever erected on the site was a Greek Orthodox monastery, built in 1892. "From here," Abaddon thought, "I will stage my revenge."

"Baal!" Abaddon summoned. "Baal!"

Baal appeared without hesitation, as if he had anticipated his master's summons. "Yes, my Lord?"

"I have a plan. A most insidious plan. Assemble the legion. We have work to do."

"Yes, my Lord." Baal vanished to do Abaddon's bidding; calling the legion to Hell's Great Hall.

chapter

FOUR

How beautiful you are, my darling; How beautiful you are!
Your eyes are like doves behind your veil...

- Song of Solomon 4:1

"I would love to stay with you longer, but I must be off to the dig site before dusk," Proudman told the *Radiant* missionaries. "Where has the day gone?"

"Where <u>had</u> the day gone?" Proudman thought to himself. He had done much of the sharing, but this group had given him something in return; a realization that there were others equally committed to the same mission. He felt re-energized. And then there was the miraculous appearance of Angelica, not in his dreams, but here, in this life and in flesh and blood. He hadn't had the opportunity to really speak to her, but they had stayed close to each other all day. Through lunch they sat side-by-side, sharing an orange and a bag of chips, while making small talk with the rest of the group. They had looked at each other the whole time and she had smiled shyly at him most of the day. But Proudman wanted to speak to her one on one. He had to know if she was feeling the same connection he was feeling.

"Angelica," Proudman turned to her and looked directly into her face. She didn't shy away.

"Yes?"

"I've wanted to get you aside all day. I think there's something between us, a connection of some kind..." Proudman spoke slowly and directly, hoping that Angelica would sense his necessity. "If I could only find the words to express to you how amazing it is that I'm here, standing in front of you, speaking to you in the flesh..."

"Why don't you just take a breath and tell me what you're feeling? And then, when you're done, I'll tell you what I think about what you tell me, and then tell you what I'm feeling."

"Sounds like a good plan," Proudman was relieved that she was taking all of this so sensibly. "So for quite some time now, I have been visited in my dreams by a woman who looks exactly, and I mean exactly, like you. She sounds like you, she has your mannerisms, and her name is even Angelica!" Proudman searched Angelica's eyes for signs of flight. "I know it's looney-tunes, but it's the God's honest truth."

"Go on..."

"I believe that God was telling me, in those dreams, to be watchful for a specific woman."

"Specific for what?"

Proudman blushed a little. "Specific for me. As a partner. For life...and stuff." He looked at Angelica's feet sheepishly.

"Wow." Was all Angelica could manage. "So you believe that God gave you prophetic dreams about me because we are supposed to be together?"

"Yeah, that about sums it up, although it didn't seem all that crazy to me until you read it back to me just now."

"Ok. So what do you want to do about it?" Angelica smiled.

"Really? I mean you're willing to entertain the possibility that there's something to all of this?" Proudman was both relieved and amazed.

"Let's just say that I find you to be...credible. And interesting. And funny. And a little bit attractive." Angelica's soft smile had turned into a full-on grin.

"Oh just a little bit attractive? What about stoically handsome? With chiseled features and stunning good looks?" Proudman chuckled.

"Maybe," Angelica teased and laughed loudly.

Proudman loved the sound of her laughter, especially now that he was hearing it live, with his ears instead of his imagination. "Praise God," he thought to himself as he watched her laughing. "Praise God from whom all blessings...this one most of all...flow."

"So, Angelica, come with me to the dig at Mt. Herod. It will give us an opportunity to get to know each other and I would love for you to meet Simon and Rachel." He looked expectantly into her eyes. "Say yes. It'll be a great adventure!"

Angelica's mind went racing. She really barely knew him. But she was definitely attracted to him. "What would the group think? But then who cares what they think," she reasoned. "There has to be something to this. God has revealed things to this man on a grand scale, so is it so terribly far-fetched that He would reveal this special relationship to him as well?" Angelica's mind was crunching all the variables when into her thoughts a still, small voice interjected, "Child, be still and trust in your heart. This man is one of mine, as are you. You certainly needn't fear him. His love for you is of me. Go. Be blessed."

"Yes." She blurted. "Yes!" Angelica was thrilled and displayed her enthusiasm outwardly. The rest of the group looked up from whatever they were doing to see what the excitement was about. "Yes! I'll go with you!" She hugged him. "Let me throw some stuff in a bag."

Proudman watched her as she ran to her tent. He laughed openly as he saw her disappear inside. Looking around at the missionaries, all wondering what was happening, Proudman blushed and offered, "I'm just going to borrow her for a few days. Going to the dig site. Gonna meet some old friends...stuff like that...it'll be fine...she'll be fine...really."

Hell's Great Hall was cavernous. From the depths of the abyss, the cavern emerged out of the blackness, as if there were a gradual transition from nothingness to permanence and structure. Despair hung from the ceiling like stalactites. Demons of stone, carved from the very walls, stared menacingly out into the immense, dark space. Burning oily pots, randomly covering the walls and floor, provided dim illumination and filled the air with foul fumes. Faint wails drifted into the hall from the bottom of the abyss; tortured souls pleading for mercy that would never come.

The blackness at the end of the Great Hall began to move, as gradually the demonic legion crawled from the abyss and entered the cavern. Floor, walls and ceiling, every inch was covered and alive, as scores of demons obediently responded to Baal's summons. All faced the hall's end opposite the abyss, where a great stone altar stood. And behind the altar, a massive rock throne, flanked on either side by terrible stone dogs, fangs bared in carved stone snarls.

Silently the demons settled in and waited for their master to appear. Baal stood next to the altar, watching the great doors in anticipation. As time passed, the demons grew restless, growling and snapping at one another until the heavy doors began to slowly and noisily open. Baal raised his hands. On cue, the demons broke into shrieks and howls and applause as Abaddon entered the Great Hall.

Abaddon strode to the throne commandingly and turned to survey his kingdom before he sat. Baal let the cacophony continue for a while longer, looking at Abaddon for a sign that the adoration had been sufficient. Abaddon nodded and Baal dropped his arms. Instantly the din ceased.

"Dark-hearted demons, fallen angels, shadowy creatures of the abyss! Hear me! For too long the so-called 'saved' humans have paid homage to God. They are a scourge and a pox on my kingdom and I can bear it no longer. They cling to their Christ and drive us from their dwelling places and, even worse, from their hearts. Their pristine souls taunt me and scoff at me...But that ends today!"

Baal raised his arms and the howls and shrieks explod-ed in approval. Abaddon raised his hand and once again the hall fell silent. "Today we will begin our attack on the saved using the bodies and minds of the unsaved; control-ling them to do our bidding and to wreak havoc in every corner of the earth. How will we infiltrate them, you ask? By entering their world of light through its most cursed and darkest places! And once establishing a foothold in those places, by ravishing the souls of the unprotected humans, those not yet claimed by God, and inhabiting their bodies, making them weapons of blessed revenge, sweet violence and joyous destruction! An army of the possessed! A le-gion of demons in human guise! It's brilliant! Worship me! My will be done!" The demons needed no prodding. They erupted in genuine approval at Abaddon's diabolical genius. "My will be done! MY WILL BE DONE ON EARTH AS IT IS IN HELL!!" The Great Hall shook in pandemonium. Hell's fury...unbridled.

Abaddon nodded to Baal, who instinctively knew that meant he was to remain and give the specific instructions. Abaddon left the Great Hall, immensely pleased with him-self, as the riotous cheering continued.

Baal began to speak and the demons' revelry subsided. "Each of you will be assigned a specific portal into the world of the living. Each of you will have a window in which to transition from spirit to a random human host. Be warned, attempting to enter the body of a child of God will prove futile and may result in your being instantly banished back to the abyss. Failure to complete your transition will meet with harsh consequences upon your return, so do not fail. Make no mistake...this is spiritual warfare...and there are souls to be won, but the main objective is revenge through the ultimate destruction of the armies of the soldiers for Christ!"

The legion once again raised their voices in approval. "Hail Abaddon! Death to Christians! Death to Jews! Victory to the powers of darkness!"

Geoffrey and Angelica departed the *Radiant* missionary camp by the pool at Lower Herodium and made their way around the base of Mt. Herod to the Hebrew University base camp. It was not a long walk, but the rocky terrain made for a slow, cautious trip unless one wanted a turned ankle or worse. It had been nearly two months since Geoffrey had left the dig site to evangelize the people of *The Gathering*. Not much had changed in the camp, although there were some differences. Under a large awning next to the operations tent, there were workers carefully building custom wooden crates in which to pack artifacts that had been discovered during the excavation of Herodium. Each relic was carefully catalogued, photographed and tagged before it was packed away for shipment to the University for study.

The sun was setting now, so Proudman knew that he would most likely find Simon and Rachel in the mess tent, sipping a cup of tea, and waiting for the evening meal to be served. To his delight, as he and Angelica entered the tent, he saw the pair with backs toward him, sitting across from Moishe Silbermann, at the usual table. Moishe looked up from his conversation and grinned widely upon recognizing Proudman.

"The prodigal son returns!" Moishe exclaimed in a thick German-Jewish accent. "And he brings with him a beautiful guest!"

Rachel turned and bolted from her seat, squealing with delight as she ran to Geoffrey and hugged his neck enthusiastically. Simon rose and walked toward Proudman with his arms open wide in greeting. "Padre! How excellent it is to see you! It has been far too long, indeed!"

"Indeed it has, my friend! Indeed it has!" Geoffrey smiled broadly and embraced his friend tightly, clapping his back as they hugged. It was, without a doubt, good to see Simon and Rachel again. Geoffrey knew he had missed their companionship, but seeing them again reinforced just how much.

"Simon. Rachel. I want you to meet...Angelica." Geoffrey reached for Angelica's hand and pulled her gently forward so that she was squarely by his side.

"Angelica?" Simon looked at her and then back at Geoffrey in disbelief. "The Angelica?"

"Yes!" Geoffrey replied emphatically.

"Your dream girl?" Rachel asked, her face clearly showing her amazement.

Angelica smiled awkwardly and felt a little bit on display.

Sensing her discomfort, Simon directed his eyes into hers. "Angelica, please forgive us and please forgive our...er, ah...amazement. You see, Geoffrey had told us about you... well, about his dreams about you, anyway, and it is just so... so...amazing that you are here, in Israel, at our dig, standing next to Geoffrey..."

"...and holding his hand!" Rachel finished Simon's sentence.

Geoffrey squeezed Angelica's hand a little tighter.

"I understand," Angelica offered. "I'm a bit amazed at all of it myself. It's all very strange and all very exciting too. Amazing!" Angelica was suddenly hyper-aware of the recurrence of forms of the word *amaze* in their conversation.

"So, welcome, Angelica...and so very pleased to meet you!" Simon hugged her and kissed her cheek.

"Yes, welcome. Very excited to meet you, Angelica!" Rachel added her hug to Simon's and kissed Angelica's cheek.

"Well, let me have a go at her!" Moishe moved in to hug Angelica and to kiss both of her cheeks. Then, holding Angelica's hands in his at arm's length, Moishe looked her over. "Reverend, you have out done yourself with this one! What a beauty you are, my child!"

Angelica blushed at Moishe's attention.

"Angelica, this is Moishe Silbermann, one of Simon's oldest and dearest friends...and one of my dearest friends as well." Geoffrey patted Moishe's shoulder as he spoke. "I have no doubt he will become one of your dearest friends also. He does that to people."

"I will grow on you." Moishe confessed to Angelica. Turning to Geoffrey, Moishe quipped, "I don't think even my dream girls measure up to her reality, Padre. You certainly can dream them up though! Maybe you could dream one up for me next time?"

The reunited group had a good laugh together as Simon motioned everyone back to the table. "It is so good to be together again!" Simon said as they sat down.

"Yes, just a couple of us are missing though," Moishe sadly commented.

"Any word from Jordan?" Geoffrey asked.

"Not since he took news of Miriam to her parents in Palestine." Rachel answered.

"Jordan Goldberg, our friend and an archaeologist with the University," Geoffrey explained to Angelica, "... and Miriam Amiran, our dear friend and Moishe's executive assistant who was gunned down on the mountain during our search for the scrolls."

Angelica nodded her understanding in appreciation of Geoffrey's desire to bring her into the group's confidence.

"Such a tragic waste. I pray Jordan is ok," Geoffrey said in a concerned tone. "And, I pray for her parents."

"It has been a long road to discovery. Indeed. A very long road," Simon stated. All nodded in silent agreement.

"Well," Moishe attempted to lift the tone. "Much good has come from all of this."

"Of that there is no doubt, my friend!" Simon agreed, lifting his spirits intentionally. "So let's once again share a meal and enjoy one another's company. And, let's hear how the good Padre found the beautiful Angelica!"

"Dying to hear this!" Rachel agreed.

As plates and bowls were placed in front of them, full of steaming, deliciously fragrant foods, Geoffrey began to tell his friends about his finding Angelica in the midst of the remnant of *The Gathering*. It was comfortable; as if no time had passed. They were friends reunited with a common purpose and the bond between them had never been stronger. Adding to their strength was Angelica, with her enthusiasm for her faith. As the friends prayed and began their meal, they had no idea how that bond would serve them in the days to come.

chapter

FIVE

Beware of the false prophets, who come to you in sheep's clothing, but inwardly are ravenous wolves.

- Matthew 7:15

ST. ONUPHRIUS MONASTERY. VALLEY OF HINNOM. HAKELDAMA.

Father Kamal Amman was disgruntled. He crumpled the paper in his clenched fist and muttered indignantly to himself. "Passed over again. It's because I'm not one of them," he reasoned. "It's because I'm not Greek. Arrogant bastards!" He tossed the wadded letter at the waste basket and watched disappointedly as it bounced off the rim and across the stone floor of his tiny room.

As Father Superior of St. Onuphrius Monastery for more than five years, Kamal Amman felt he had earned his stripes. A Palestinian by birth, Amman had joined the Greek Orthodox Church forty years ago as a young man, forced into a life of service by an overbearing mother soon after the death of his father. In his mind, he had served as deacon, parish priest, monk, archpriest, archmonk and now Father Superior, all with more than satisfactory performance. It was time for him to be Bishop.

"Running a high-profile Jerusalem tourist attraction, which also happens to be a church and monastery, is no easy task," he had complained to the Archbishop. "But I do it and I do it without complaining," he had insisted.

"You have no patience," the Archbishop had replied. "And, you should perhaps pray and explore your motives, Kamal. They sound to me to be rather...un-bishop-like."

"Un-bishop-like!" Amman said out loud as he recalled the conversation. And now this latest letter confirmed it; he would not be promoted this year. "Damn," he muttered. "Better I had never embarked on this path all those years ago. Better I had disobeyed my mother, may she rot. Better I had followed Islam like a normal Arab. Better I had bowed down to Satan himself!"

Kamal felt it immediately upon saying the words. There was a noticeable heaviness in his tiny room; as if the air had been suddenly sucked out and had been replaced by something of greater density. The single bulb over head flickered and then remained lit, although with much less intensity than before. Kamal noticed he could see his breath when he exhaled. He backed anxiously toward the door, wanting nothing more than to flee whatever was happening in his room. Frost formed on metal surfaces. As he reached back for the door handle, he felt an icy chill on his neck just before something hit him hard from behind. Whatever had hold of him gripped him brutally and drove him into the opposite wall with tremendous force. Kamal tried to scream, but there was no air in his lungs to achieve the desired result. His face was held mercilessly against the rough stone wall with such pressure that Kamal was certain his cheek bones would shatter at any moment. His teeth cut into the inside of his mouth and he tasted his own blood. Fear controlled him completely.

As Kamal remained held by the unseen force, he could not recall even a single word of prayer. His thoughts were jumbled and he could do nothing but whimper. Then he felt the intrusion, as if his mind and body were slowly being pulled apart. Out of the corner of his eye, Kamal saw dark, shadowy figures approaching from behind. He felt a dark presence enter him, pushing him out of his own body. As he emerged, the shadowy figures grabbed hold of him and began pulling and tugging at him in an effort to remove him more efficiently from his body. More and more violently, the figures ripped his soul free, while the intruder from within pushed him out.

All at once the violent extraction stopped. Kamal stared in horrid disbelief at his body staring back at him with black soulless eyes. The demon inside his body smiled at him with his own face. It was not like any smile Kamal had ever seen in the mirror.

"What do you want with me?" Kamal heard himself sob.

"Only your body..." the demon said back to him. Kamal tried to wrap his mind around the raspy voice, not his own, coming out of what until mere minutes ago was his mouth. "And your soul, of course," the demon added.

As the shadows pulled Kamal roughly out of the room, and out of the world of the living, the demon inside Kamal's body licked the blood from the inside of his lips and savored its metallic sweetness and saltiness together. The tiny room filled with maniacal chuckling as the demon moved to the mirror on Kamal's wall, admiring his new body, flexing his arms and fingers in rapturous delight.

The evening was winding down at the base camp as Simon, Rachel, Moishe, Geoffrey and Angelica sat in the coolness of the operations tent enjoying coffee and conversation.

"Simon...Rachel...when I left the dig two months ago, you two were talking about a wedding, I recall, yes?" Geoffrey looked at them with anticipation.

"Indeed," responded Simon. "And, that is still the plan, Reverend. Isn't it, my love?" Simon reached for Rachel's hand.

"Yes it is!" Rachel agreed as her hand met Simon's. "Know any good priests?"

"As a matter of fact I do!" Geoffrey volunteered. "I'm free for the next few days if you want to make it official," Geoffrey prodded.

"You know, Simon, we could go ahead and do it." Rachel turned to Simon and the two began a conversation as if they were suddenly the only two people in the room.

"Nothing would make me happier, but are you sure you don't want the dress, and the flowers, and the church, and all the accoutrements?" Simon wanted to please her.

"Those things are nice, but they are certainly not what make a wedding special. We have our friends here. Except Jordan, of course, but we can try and reach him. And, we have a priest, and I'm sure Angelica wouldn't mind being my maid of honor. And Moishe would obviously be your best man." Rachel said matter-of-factly.

"Indeed."

"Simon, really...give me more feedback than 'Indeed.'" Rachel insisted.

Simon grinned. "I say we do it now. We try and reach Jordan tomorrow and then we do it the day after, whether we reach him or not!"

Geoffrey, Angelica and Moishe sat with faces beaming as they witnessed the couple interact. Moishe broke in first. "Splendid! I will have my caterers do the reception in the mess tent! There will be wine, hors d'œuvres, table linens, silverware...an incredible feast...the works! You won't even know you are in the desert!"

"Oh, but Simon," Rachel grasped Simon's arm. "We don't have wedding bands!"

"Hmm," Simon responded thoughtfully. "That's not entirely accurate, my love." Simon reached into the cargo pocket of his khakis and pulled out a dark green velvet box. In one motion, he moved it directly in front of Rachel while flipping the lid open, revealing gleaming platinum rings. "I picked them up on my last run into Jerusalem. I thought they might come in handy."

Rachel was floored. "Simon, they're absolutely beautiful...breathtaking...really!" She leaned in to kiss him. Simon met her half way. "What on earth could have made this moment more perfect?" She said into Simon's eyes.

"Perhaps this?" Simon reached back into his cargo pocket and extracted a second box, smaller, but similar in color and texture. Holding the box in front of Rachel, he again flipped open the lid. The room seemed to brighten as the light danced off of the round, solitaire diamond. Simon searched Rachel's eyes for approval.

Rachel's hands trembled their way to her mouth. Tears welled up in her eyes and then streaked down her face. She was speechless.

"I think she likes it." Angelica reassured Simon.

Simon was not reassured and sat holding the ring while Rachel continued to cry. "Are those happy tears, my love?" Simon finally asked tentatively.

"Yes, Simon...yes...very happy tears." Rachel fanned her face with her hands. "It is magnificent, Simon...stunningly magnificent. Thank you!"

"Well, let's put it on that finger, shall we?" Simon removed the ring from the slot while Rachel extended her fingers in anticipation of receiving the ring. Simon gently held Rachel's hand and carefully slid the diamond onto her slender finger. "Good," he said in relief. "It fits!"

"Look at that rock!" Geoffrey taunted. "Where did you dig that treasure up, Simon?"

"No, my friend...someone else did the digging for this artifact!" Simon fired back.

"It's gorgeous." Angelica admired Rachel's extended hand. "Congratulations you two."

"Yes, congratulations!" Moishe chimed in. "And now a toast!" Moishe raised his coffee cup. The group responded by raising their cups. Moishe proceeded, "To my dearest friend and his beautiful bride to be; May your marriage be long and full of joy. May your house be blessed and may the Holy Spirit always reside there! Mazel tov!"

"Mazel tov!" The group enthusiastically responded.

The demon in Kamal's body quickly grew bored of admiring himself in the mirror. He moved from the mirror to the crucifix hanging on the opposite wall. The demon sniffed at it in a dog-like fashion and growled a low rumbling growl. He then removed the cross from the wall and replaced it upside-down before backing away and settling in a corner of the room.

Focusing on the inverted crucifix, the demon entered into a trance-like state to communicate with his master. "My Lord, I am here to do your bidding." In his mind, he repeated the phrase like a mantra. "My Lord, I am here to do your bidding. My Lord, I am here to do your bidding..."

chapter

SIX

'The wedding is ready, but those who were invited were not worthy.

Go therefore to the main highways, and as many as you find there, invite to the wedding feast.'

- Matthew 22:8-9

Moishe Silbermann boarded his Land Rover and left the base camp for Jerusalem. It was early and the morning sun was just turning the horizon hues of pink and purple. His plan was to drive to his bistro and get his head chef going on the menu for Simon and Rachel's wedding. There was no time to waste if he were to pull off this feast in time.

He was not at all sure that his food distributors and suppliers had survived the Islamic Alliance's attack on the city. To be certain, regular service would be slow if not altogether cut off. All over Jerusalem, clean up and rebuilding were making progress, but normalcy was still months away.

"Such an ugly business...war," Moishe said to himself. His thoughts immediately went to Miriam. "Such a senseless waste of a beautiful life," he thought. She was not the only executive assistant Moishe had employed over the years, but she was the only one he had grown to love. She had become like a daughter to him, and he had become a father figure to her.

"Moishe Silbermann," she would scold him affectionately, "you need to take better care of yourself. You eat too much and exercise too little!" She was the only one who could get away with telling him what to do. "I want you to be around for my wedding, God willing I should ever find the right man to marry." Moishe chuckled in a melancholy way.

"Not a one of them out there good enough for you, my sweet," he would say in response. It was a usual game and they enjoyed the comfortable, affectionate repetition of it.

Moishe's thoughts turned to Jordan Goldberg. Jordan and Miriam were just beginning to develop into a couple when Miriam was killed. It was Jordan who had carried Miriam's lifeless body off of the mountain all the way to the base camp, refusing help when it was offered. And, it was Jordan who carried the terrible news of Miriam's death home to Palestine; home to her parents. Moishe wondered how that sad evolution had gone. He looked at his mobile phone and was pleasantly surprised to see that he had a signal. It had been several weeks since he had seen signal bars on his phone, most of the towers having been knocked out during the bombardment. Moishe dialed Jordan's number. The Bluetooth system in the Land Rover came to life and he heard ringing through the onboard speakers.

"Hello?" It was Jordan's sleepy voice.

"Good morning, young professor!" Moishe was glad to hear Jordan's voice. "Did I wake you?"

"Moishe, my friend...yes, yes you did wake me, but it's a good thing because my sleep has been plagued with nightmares. I keep reliving the loss of my Miriam...over and over in my dreams."

"I was wondering how you were coping."

"I'm coping, just not living."

"How are Miriam's parents taking all of this?"

"They took it very hard, Moishe. They were so reluctant to let her leave the nest in the first place, and now their worst fears are their reality. They've been really good to me though...treat me like family...like a son."

"I really think you would have been, given the time to...sorry."

"I know...it's ok, Moishe. I think Miriam and I would've been great together. But, sadly...it was just not to be."

"Well, I have some good news if you are up to it."

"I don't recall what that feels like, but let me have it."

"Simon and Rachel are getting married in two days on top of Mt. Herod. They are hoping that you will be there, in fact, they would be extremely disappointed if you were not there."

"Far be it from me to disappoint on such a happy occasion, Moishe. I'll be there. I'll leave today. I suppose it's about time I rejoined the living."

"That's the spirit, young professor! That's the spirit! I'll see you at the dig. Much preparation to be done. I've a feast to plan!"

"Excellent, Moishe. I'm sure it will be grand. And Moishe..."

"Yes, Jordan?"

"Thank you for allowing me to take care of Miriam. I know you loved her too."

"She was like my very own daughter. But, even I could tell that she was falling for you and, just so you know...you were...are...the only one who I ever thought was worthy of the special woman she was."

"Thank you my friend. That means more than you know. See you soon."

"Safe travels, young professor."

Moishe depressed the call cancel button on the Land Rover's steering wheel, as he rolled into the outskirts of Jerusalem. Construction equipment passed him going the opposite direction, hauling debris to a land fill. The city skyline still looked beautiful despite the heavy destruction inflicted by the Alliance. Moishe wondered how magnificent the New Jerusalem of the scriptures would be if it were truly more incredible than the city that spanned before him. This was home. Moishe loved it so.

Geoffrey made his way to the field showers; one of the things he liked best about the base camp. Solar water heaters and huge, black, rubber, heat-absorbing water bladders made for plenty of hot water courtesy of the sun's radiant energy. The anticipation of a hot shower made Geoffrey whistle happily as he traversed the camp.

Angelica stirred in her cot as the whistling invaded her sub consciousness. Her eyelashes fluttered and she slowly opened her sleepy blue eyes, glancing blurrily at her watch and then raising her head from her pillow high enough to peer out the mesh window at the head of her cot. Her eyes zeroed in on the source of the whistling as Proudman passed her tent.

"Where ya headed, Padre?" she called through the window.

Geoffrey stopped and turned toward Angelica's voice, seeing only her outline through the mesh window. "Shower!" he answered.

"Really? There's a shower here?" Angelica grew excited about the possibility of getting actual shampoo in her hair and soap on her skin.

"Yup. His and hers. Grab your towel and I'll show you where."

"Hot water?"

"More than you could ever use!"

"I might surprise you. I can use a lot...shampoo, rinse and repeat, shaving these long legs, then just general lathering and rinsing; I'm good for a few gallons, easily."

"I think we can handle it. Come on!"

"Be right there!"

Geoffrey watched as Angelica emerged from her tent with a towel draped around her neck. Her hair was tussled a bit and her over-sized University of Texas t-shirt looked like a burnt-orange mini dress. Proudman thought he felt his heart rate increase.

"So what's with the whistling so early in the morning, Padre? Got something to be happy about?"

"Just happy with the way things are, I guess," Geoffrey smiled at her.

"This is the day the Lord hath made. Let us rejoice and be glad in it."

"Exactly."

"So, what's the plan for the day?" Angelica asked lightly.

"Well, after showers...breakfast. And then, I thought we could hike to the top of the mountain and look for the best place to hold a wedding. On the way, I thought of stopping at Miriam's grave and saying a prayer for her. And after that, well, I suppose I haven't thought that far ahead. Is there anything special you'd like to do?"

"I'm not on a schedule for the next few days. I thought we could just wing it and see where God takes us. I'd just like to get to know who you are...ya know?"

"I like that. Then that's the plan...we just won't have a plan."

"I concur, counselor!" Angelica smiled and reached for Geoffrey's hand as they approached the field showers.

"Girls to the left, boys to the right," Geoffrey motioned.

"K. See you after." Angelica's hand lingered in Geoffrey's until the last possible moment as she entered the shower tent. Geoffrey's gaze followed her until the spring-loaded door closed behind her.

The demonic Kamal continued his mantra, "My Lord, I am here to do your bidding. My Lord, I am here to do your bidding..." As he chanted, the mirror began to develop a coating of frost. The temperature in the tiny chamber dropped and the demon's hot breath looked like smoke as he exhaled.

All at once the bed began to shake and bounce off of the floor violently. Drawers flew from their resting places in the dresser and writing desk and crashed loudly into the stone walls, splintering upon impact. The inverted crucifix on the wall fell to the floor with a clatter and the mirror cracked diagonally from corner to corner. As the crack raced across the reflective surface, a pale hand jutted out of the fissure. Then an arm, and a leg, until the figure of Abaddon himself stood in the physical world.

Demon Kamal fell on his face at Abaddon's pale, bare feet. "Master," he said reverently.

"You have done well, child."

"It is my honor to serve you, Master."

"Yes. Yes it is."

"What is your bidding, Master?"

"My bidding? Only this, my child..." Abaddon motioned for Demon Kamal to rise. As he did so, Abaddon thrust his pale hand violently into the demon's chest. The sudden penetration shocked the demon at first, and then the pain registered in his brain, causing him to shriek and squirm. Abaddon thrust just as violently with a second hand, plunging it into Demon Kamal's body right next to the first hand. The demon looked into Abaddon's eyes in questioning disbelief. Abaddon spread his hands apart and the demon's human chest split. The demon went limp and Abaddon pulled Kamal's body on as if he were putting on a sport coat, expelling the inhabitant in the process.

"But Master," the replaced demon protested, "I have served you well."

"That you have child, and now your usefulness is finished. Be gone, back to Hell with you. This body is mine. My revenge is personal. I will handle this myself."

The dejected demon retreated through the crack in the mirror, wailing in anguish as he went. Abaddon touched the gaping wound in Kamal's body, healing the tissue as he traced the torn flesh with his finger tips. Kamal's mouth smiled wickedly and the brown pigment in his eyes turned jet black, like the abyss.

chapter

SEVEN

When I saw Him, I fell at His feet like a dead man. And He placed His right hand on me, saying, "Do not be afraid; I am the first and the last,

and the living One; and I was dead, and behold, I am alive forevermore, and I have the keys of death and of Hades.

- Revelation 1:17-18

Geoffrey felt rejuvenated. The warmth of the shower, the scent of the soap, the abundance of water had made a new man of him. He hastily dressed, anxious to start his day with Angelica. As he fumbled with the buttons on his shirt, he silently thanked God for bringing her into his life after so many years of waiting.

"Lord," he prayed, "Your ways are a mystery to me. Your wisdom is far beyond my understanding. Your timing is all Your own, and perfect. Your grace is reflective of Your generosity and Your mercy. Just and compassionate is Your loving kindness, my God. And, I, Your servant, though undeserving on my own merit, appreciate the blessing You pour upon me in the form of Angelica."

Proudman finished dressing and trotted across the way to Angelica's tent. Angelica was just brushing her hair and checking herself in the small mirror suspended from the tent's center support. "Wow, maybe I should have packed a little makeup for this trip," she muttered. "But then who knew I would run into a great guy in the middle of the desert?" She did have mascara and lip balm. "It'll have to do," she said, taking one last glance in the mirror before exiting the tent.

Proudman approached smiling. He watched as she once again pulled her hair into a ponytail. She was dressed in khaki shorts and a khaki blouse. Geoffrey gazed at her as if she were dressed to the nines.

"What?" Angelica said as she caught him staring.

"What?" Geoffrey responded playfully.

"You're staring." She said accusatorily.

"I'm not staring. I'm admiring."

"Stalker!" Angelica kidded.

"Guilty as charged," Geoffrey responded in kind.

Angelica laughed. She had to admit that she loved his attention. She reached for Geoffrey's hand and then clung to his arm as they began to walk toward the mess tent.

"I'm starving," Angelica offered as the smell of sausage and eggs filled her nostrils.

"It smells like breakfast is ready, and I'm ready for it," Geoffrey said emphatically. "Let's get a good breakfast and then hike up to the top for a look around."

"I'm right beside you," Angelica agreed. She leaned her head against his arm as they walked. "I'm having a really great time getting to know you and your friends," she admitted. "Simon and Rachel seem really good together."

"They absolutely are. They have such a passion for everything...passion for life, passion for their work, passion for each other, and passion...an unbelievable passion, for their Savior."

"Sounds like a great foundation for a marriage."

"The best. No doubt about it. If I ever get married again, you can bet that this time around, it will be centered in Christ. I prayed continuously that God would not let me be distracted by any woman who was not the one He had planned for me. And, in my dreams, He showed me you. So I waited for you, believing all along that when I was ready, or when you were ready, or maybe when He was ready, I would find you."

"That sounds like a prayer I should be praying right now," Angelica said honestly.

"Why do you say that?" Geoffrey was caught off guard by Angelica's words.

"I mean, I'm here in the Holy Land, on the adventure of a lifetime. And I meet a great guy who tells me that I'm the one he's been looking for all his life. Not only that, but he tells me that God revealed me to him in his dreams... dreams that were the result of countless prayers. A girl could easily get swept off her feet if she let herself."

"Afraid?"

"Got my running shoes on."

"No need for those. I'm not going to hurt you. And I'm certainly not going to attempt to pressure you into anything you are not ready for. I'm in no hurry either."

"No, I don't think you are going to hurt me...I just haven't had tremendous success in relationships. So I'm a bit gun shy."

"Not to worry. Let's just take our time and see where God leads us. In fact, let's make each other a promise...that we will seek God first in all things. That He will have control of our relationship from this day forward. And that our trust will be placed squarely in Him so that we can always trust in each other. Ok?"

"Ok."

"Alright then, let's make it official. I promise."

"And I promise too."

"Good."

Geoffrey reached for the screen door to the mess tent and opened it for Angelica. "Thank you, sir," she said, gliding past him and planting a kiss on his unsuspecting lips as she passed.

"You're welcome," Proudman said in a daze. A grin broke out on his face as he followed Angelica into the tent.

Simon looked at Rachel wanting to know if she had also seen Angelica's affectionate gesture. Rachel sat gleaming as she watched Angelica enter the mess tent with Geoffrey following her, grinning ear-to-ear.

"Well, good morning," Rachel said smiling like a cat.

"What?" Angelica said defensively.

"You seem to be warming up to the whole Geoffrey experience," Rachel teased.

"Yeah, well...a girl has to do what a girl has to do."

"Indeed." Simon offered his assessment of Angelica's defense.

Geoffrey sat down across from Simon, still grinning broadly.

"You seem rather pleased with things this morning, Padre," Simon goaded.

"Pleased? Indeed." Geoffrey borrowed Simon's trademark expression. "Indeed."

Simon could not contain a hearty laugh. "Angelica, my dear, you have done with a single kiss what none of us have ever been able to do...render the good reverend speechless."

"Well, let me know if he starts to bother you with his constant talking. I'll be more than happy to shut him up again." Angelica truly felt a part of the group now, and her delightful wit and personality shined.

"Perfect!" Simon said excitedly. "By George, I like her, Padre!" Simon clapped Geoffrey on the shoulder.

The foursome shared breakfast and connected. They were friends. They rejoiced in their time together. As they were in fellowship, Geoffrey reminded each of them that they were living out the scriptures in the 2nd chapter of Acts:

Day by day continuing with one mind in the temple, and breaking bread from house to house, they were taking their meals together with gladness and sincerity of heart,

praising God and having favor with all the people. And the Lord was adding to their number day by day those who were being saved.

Moishe pulled the Land Rover up to the front of his bistro. Thankfully, it had been spared any major damage from the Islamic Alliance's onslaught. His wait staff was busily wiping down the courtyard tables and replacing the shrapnel riddled umbrellas. He greeted each one of them individually, grateful that each one had been spared, asking each of them about their families and homes.

As he made his way to the kitchen, he stopped at each person he met, hugging them and asking them how they had fared during the attack. Finally reaching the kitchen, he found Joseph, his chef, and embraced him.

"Joseph, Joseph, I am so very glad you are safe!"

"Moishe, you are well, praise God in heaven!"

"Your family?"

"All well, my friend."

"And you, Moishe? How are you?"

"I'm good. You know, of course, that we lost our dear Miriam?"

"Yes, I had heard. We were deeply saddened, and we worried about you having to deal with her loss by yourself. We had tried to get you to evacuate with us, but when we stopped by your home, you were not there, my friend."

"No. But no worries. I was with friends and safe in the arms of God."

"Good, my friend. And it is good to be back at work."

"Well, I have plenty of work for you, Joseph. I need you to create a wedding menu. I want you to spare no expense and pull out all the stops. Finest of everything."

"That may be easier said than done, my friend. The distributors are slow to recover and the marketplace was badly hit."

"I thought that might be the case, but do your best. If you need wine, get it from my personal cellar. My dearest friends are getting married in two days and I want to make it a special event."

"I will make it a grand feast, my friend. You have my word."

"Then it will be so, Joseph. I have always known your word to be true. God bless you, my friend. I praise Him that you are safe and well."

"Likewise, my friend. Leave everything to me."

Geoffrey and Angelica left the mess tent and walked hand in hand toward the road leading to the top of Mt. Herod. Their mood was light and they walked in silence as they enjoyed each other's company. Geoffrey was surprised at how comfortable the silence seemed. There was no awkwardness, nor was there the urge to fill the quiet with trivial talk. The sound of their footsteps in the gravel and the contentment of just being together was enough.

As they reached the site of Miriam's grave, they stopped to pay their respects. The grave was lined with local stones and a cross carved from the ancient stone of Herodium stood as the headstone. Native shrubs and an olive tree adorned the area, all newly planted to mark Miriam's memorial.

The couple stood reverently, and Geoffrey began to recite from memory.

"I am Resurrection and I am Life, says the Lord. Whoever has faith in me shall have life, even though he die. And everyone who has life, and has committed himself to me in faith, shall not die for ever.

As for me, I know that my Redeemer lives and that at the last he will stand upon the earth. After my awaking, he will raise me up; and in my body I shall see God. I myself shall see, and my eyes behold him who is my friend and not a stranger.

For none of us has life in himself, and none becomes his own master when he dies. For if we have life, we are alive in the Lord, and if we die, we die in the Lord. So, then, whether we live or die, we are the Lord's possession.

Happy from now on are those who die in the Lord! So it is, says the Spirit, for they rest from their labors."

"That's beautiful," Angelica whispered. "What's that from?"

"Burial Rite II," Geoffrey answered, "from the *Book of Common Prayer.*"

"It reminds me of the Catholic liturgy of my youth."

Geoffrey nodded in acknowledgement and prayed a blessing over Miriam's grave, *"O God, whose blessed Son was laid in a sepulcher in the garden: Bless we pray, this grave, and grant that she whose body is buried here may dwell with Christ in paradise, and may come to your heavenly kingdom; through your Son Jesus Christ our Lord. Amen."*

"Amen," Angelica responded.

Geoffrey took Angelica's hand and the two turned away to continue their hike to the top. They walked to the summit, neither one feeling the need to speak. Peace settled in both of their hearts. They knew Miriam was happy and well in heaven. And they knew that all things had indeed worked together for good and for the glory of God the Father.

chapter

EIGHT

For Topheth has long been ready, Indeed, it has been prepared for the king. He has made it deep and large, A pyre of fire with plenty of wood; The breath of the LORD, like a torrent of brimstone, sets it afire.

- Isaiah 30:33

Abaddon, in Kamal's body, made his way to the monastery's business office. His dark mind churned as he worked out the details of his revenge. How would he get those responsible for *The Gathering* to assemble within striking distance of his new guise as Father Superior of St. Onuphrius? What would interest them enough to drop whatever they were doing and converge on his monastery? It would have to be an incredible ruse. But what?

"They are archaeologists," Abaddon reasoned. "So, a find of great magnitude and significance might gain their attention." But, what could he give them that would be a greater draw than Herodium? "Perhaps not an actual find," he thought, "but the appearance of a find; a grand deception!"

Abaddon knew the area around Hakeldama extremely well. For thousands of years his influence in the Valley of Hinnom had produced the most gruesome and cruel horrors. If the Temple Mount was the domain of God in Jerusalem, then the Hinnom Valley was Satan's playground—Hell on earth. He would use his familiarity with the valley, and its dark past, to his advantage. He reached for the phone on his desk.

"Archbishop Charalampous, please," Abaddon said in Kamal's best business-like tone. "Yes, thank you. Please tell him Father Kamal Amman is calling from St. Onuphrius."

"Charalampous here. Is that you Father Amman?"

"Yes, Your Eminence, it is I"

"What can I do for you, Kamal?"

"I need your...guidance. It seems we have stumbled on to something here at the monastery...a find of some significance...an ancient tomb beneath the monastery."

"Kamal, there must be thirty or forty tombs in your immediate vicinity. What is so significant about finding yet another one?"

"This one is...different. Early Christian symbols everywhere. There are indications that the remains may be those of one of the twelve apostles. I recommend we get someone well qualified to assess what we have here."

"I will call someone..."

"Your Eminence, might I suggest a better solution?"

"I'm listening, Kamal."

"There is a world-renowned specialist working nearby at Herodium...Dr. Simon Cross. He has a team from Hebrew University working an archaeological site as we speak."

"Of course I know of Dr. Cross' work at Herodium, Kamal. His discovery is only one of the most significant finds to Christianity ever! What makes you think he would come to St. Onuphrius?"

"Well, Your Eminence...because I will send the invitation in your name, of course."

"Oh. Well, yes, of course. That should do it. Yes, by all means, Kamal. Send the invitation in my name and let me know when Dr. Cross responds. Good work. You just might make bishop after all, Kamal."

"Thank you, Your Eminence. I'll be in touch." Abaddon replaced the phone on to its base and smiled. "Your arrogance and vanity are so predictable, Charalampous. I will enjoy squeezing the life out of your worthless neck when you are no longer useful to me."

Geoffrey and Angelica reached the summit of Herodium and took in their surroundings. The grid stakes that had been used during the initial survey of the site had been removed, and the site looked as it did when Geoffrey had first seen it; before *The Gathering,* before Miriam's terrible death, before Inspector Abrahms' sacrifice for the team, before the technological miracle, ISAIAH, showed them the way to Herod's tomb, before God revealed the scrolls.

The couple walked down the entrance ramp, which was tiered in such a way that it resembled broad stairs. The ramp ended at a large stone platform, which overlooked the courtyard and atrium, deep inside Herodium's cone. Two stone staircases, one on either end of the platform, gave access to the courtyard by way of five massive stone steps on each end.

"This platform would make a nice altar for Simon and Rachel," Geoffrey offered.

"And the guests could watch from the courtyard. Everyone could see from there," Angelica added. "And, the ramp would make for a great entrance, especially if we had the wedding at dusk."

"It's perfect," Geoffrey agreed. "Considering the wonderful...and terrible...things that have happened here."

Angelica nodded in agreement. "A wedding will be refreshing."

"Yup." Geoffrey nodded.

⚘

Simon and Rachel were just leaving the mess tent when a courier from the University rolled into the camp on an all-terrain motorcycle. The courier dismounted and walked directly toward the operations tent.

"Looking for me?" Cross called after him.

The messenger turned and responded, "Are you Dr. Cross?"

"I am he."

"Urgent message for you, Doctor."

"Urgent, you say? Who's it from?"

"Not sure, Doctor. It's from the monastery in Hinnom."

"Indeed. Thank you, my good man. Get yourself some breakfast before you head back to Jerusalem." Simon motioned toward the mess tent.

"Thank you, Doctor. I think I will!" The courier moved in the direction Simon had pointed.

"Let's go to operations and take a look at this message, shall we, my love?"

"Right beside you, love," Rachel responded happily. "How excitingly cryptic!"

Geoffrey and Angelica sat together on one of the massive stone steps leading down to Herodium's atrium. He took her hand and smiled into her eyes. She smiled back.

"This is a little overwhelming," Angelica admitted.

"I figured you might be getting cold feet at some point."

"I have a habit of putting on my running shoes when relationships are too complex."

"Well, I thought a lot about that last night and I wrote some thoughts down for you...just to give you more information and maybe some peace of mind." Geoffrey reached into his pocket and pulled out several pages folded into a neat little package.

"Should I read it now?"

"If you want. I mean, it might give you some clarity."

Angelica unfolded the letter and gave Geoffrey a nervous smile before she began to read.

My Sweetest Angelica,

These past few days have been nothing short of amazing to me. I feel as if I have been watching firsthand the work of God in my life. You have touched me in such a profound way. I want you to know everything there is to know about me, so that you can see that I am truly just a simple man who is deeply committed to you, and to this relationship.

Since God is so obviously a part of this, sharing my faith story with you may be a good foundation on which to build. So...I'm inviting you on a very personal journey in the hope that it might help you find peace and reassurance (and warm feet). Writing this will be a challenge, as it is complex, but it is something important that you should know.

I'm a deeply reflective person by nature. I like to go off by myself for short periods and think about where I've been, not to dwell and wallow in it, but to learn from it; to see what it has to teach me; to see how the hand of God has moved me from the depths of despair to the relative calm I enjoy now. Reflection, in my experience, is an act of appreciation for God in my life.

When I think about it, my sweet Angelica, I sometimes identify my life with a passage of scripture that speaks as a theme of my life. For example, one such passage is from Romans 8.

It says, "Who will separate us from the love of Christ? Will tribulation, or distress, or persecution, or famine, or nakedness, or peril, or sword? Just as it is written, 'For your sake we are being put to death all day long; we were considered as sheep to be slaughtered.' But in all these things we overwhelmingly conquer through Him who loved us. For I am convinced that neither death, nor life, nor angels, nor principalities, nor things present, nor things to come, nor powers, nor height, nor depth, nor any created thing, will be able to separate us from the love of God, which is in Christ Jesus our Lord."

Angel, I was brought up in a Christian home. And because of that, I always had the perception that I was a Christian. I call that being "saved by osmosis"—where grace just seeps through your pores and you don't have to do anything—it just happens to you. But grace by osmosis is a fallacy. As I discovered in my life, Angelica, there is a required action that we all must take in order to be saved. We must ask for grace and claim the redemptive blood of Jesus as the basis for our request. It took me some hard lessons to figure that out.

My brother, Michael, and I were very close. One day, we were throwing a baseball in my mom and dad's yard. Dad was barbequing—sometimes Angelica, I swear I can still smell that smoke from the pit. My brother decided he wanted to take a ride out to Magnolia to see the new house mom and dad were in the process of buying. He asked if I wanted to go, but I said no.

So he jumped in his car...and that was the last time I saw him alive...he was killed in route by a drunk driver who ran a stop sign and plowed into him at 65 miles an hour...senseless. Here one minute...gone the next. And I was angry...at God...at myself for not going with him...at the entire world.

I was so filled with rage that nothing mattered...not family... not my future...nothing mattered. So I ran away from God and from life. I rode around the country and Canada with no direction and nothing but the clothes on my back...weeks...I checked out. I'm not proud of it, but I'm trying to be totally transparent to you.

Eventually I ended up back in Houston and parked my motorcycle in front of a Marine recruiting office. I remember the poster in the window that said, "We're looking for a few good men... with the metal to be Marines." I went in and told the Sergeant behind the desk to sign me up.

Angelica, I am convinced that the divine, merciful, loving hand of God caused me to stop exactly where I needed to be that day. The Marines gave me back a devotion to God, Country and Corps. It gave my life a purpose again. I moved through the ranks and was selected to go to Officer Candidate School when I was a Corporal. I became a Mustang (an enlisted Marine that becomes an officer) and all of it was made possible by a merciful God that didn't let go of me even when I had let go of myself.

During the Gulf War, I was assigned to lead an advance party of artillery into a position in the Al Burqan oilfields of Kuwait. The position was supposed to be free of enemy combatants, but our intelligence was wrong and as we dug in to the position we found ourselves getting hammered by tanks, artillery, mortars and rockets. My advance party was completely surrounded and caught in an intense barrage.

Enemy ran through our position and combat turned hand-to-hand. An Iraqi came at me with bayonet fixed and I climbed from my fighting hole to meet him on equal footing...my pistol was expended so I picked up a wounded Marine's rifle and fixed bayonet as well.

As the Iraqi approached, he thrust his bayonet and I deflected and countered with a slash to his neck. As he lay on the ground dying, I sat down on the sand next to him and put my hand over the gash in his neck and I felt his life slip away...blood ran through my fingers and stained the sand beneath him.

So many times, Angelica, in that brief war, I was spared. Why? I wondered. I was certainly not a saint. I was so short of the glory of God it was ridiculous. I had blood on my hands.

After the war, I was stationed in Okinawa for six months. The long year and a half away from my family followed by 6 months in Okinawa helped compound a situation where my ex became even more restless and moved on with her life...but could I really blame her? Still, I was disappointed in life. I was serving the Corps faithfully, but there was no love to hold my marriage together—maybe there never had been. And, I was longing for the relationship that I knew God had for me with someone extra special—I was longing for you, but just didn't know it yet.

The battalion Chaplain, a Catholic priest, and I became friends. One day after work I sat in his office and I began a rant about how my life was devoid of passion, how I had made so many mistakes, how I should not have married out of a sense of duty rather than love, how I had blood on my hands and could never know God's love and mercy...and on and on...

Then something happened...my friend, the priest...a man of God...grabbed my shoulders and shook me and said to me, "Be still!" Then he took the Bible from the side table and he placed it in my hand and he said these words, which will forever be ingrained in me...He said, "This is passion...this is life...full of hope...full of the promise of God's love...all you have to do is ask for it."

Angelica, I could feel the presence of God in that office. He asked me if I had ever asked Christ into my life. I had never said those words. So we said them together right there. I was saved. But, I soon learned that being saved doesn't mean your life will be trouble free from that moment on...

Not long after that, my father became ill and I made a choice to leave the Corps I loved to return home to help my mom and dad adjust. My dad didn't last long after I got home and after getting my mom situated, I began to search for what to do next.

I went to work in the airline industry. But, I sensed I had a calling elsewhere, I just wasn't sure what it was. I just knew there was something more out there. Suddenly, life as I knew it changed. One day at work I fell 22 feet from a DC-10 aircraft. I shattered my arms and wrists, fractured my hip and sustained a closed head injury that put me in a coma for 7 days. When I woke up, I had memory problems, required a speech therapist to learn to speak again and had issues that took me two full years to overcome.

That accident was the catalyst that brought me into a search for my deeper relationship with Christ. It was what put me on the path to the priesthood, which landed me in seminary and then finally as a priest in the Diocese of Texas.

Angel, God's plan for me has been in motion since before I was born. I have had choices along the way, but ultimately it's all His design. I am not on this journey alone. I can look at that scripture from Romans and I can apply it to my life...and it reads a little differently in my personal version, but the meaning is the same.

"I am convinced that neither death, nor car wrecks, nor war, nor blood on my hands, nor losing my brother to a drunk driver, nor losing my father to a dreadful illness, nor a failed loveless marriage, nor making bad choices, nor falling from airplanes, nor life , nor angels, nor principalities, nor things present, nor things to come, nor powers, nor height, nor depth, nor any created thing, will ever be able to separate me from the love of God, which is in Christ Jesus our Lord."

And now I stand here...watching my faith story continue. You are now part of it, in fact you are the reason for it all and you are *so very welcome in my life. Now I am content that I am where I am supposed to be. Every event in my life has led me here to this intersection where your life and my life meet. Chance? Hardly.*

I really needed you to see where I came from. It is my sincere desire, that you will find your way clear to one day become a permanent part of me. Until that day, rest easy in the knowledge that, for you, I have all the time and patience in the world.

And never forget, my sweetest, truest Angel...that I am forever here for you to lean on. I will gladly share your pain, your passion, your joy and your life...all of it...and any burden you want to unload onto me...I will happily carry for you.

I care for you so very deeply...

-Geoffrey

Angelica wiped tears from her cheeks. Geoffrey had been silent as she read, and he continued to be so. She looked at him and reached for his hand and said, "I can tell you this...I promise that I will leave my running shoes packed away, and I will stand with you as we figure this whole thing out."

"I could not ask for anything more." Geoffrey pulled her close to him and hugged her as they sat together, surrounded by the remnants of the ancient past, and the promise of a new, exciting future.

✺

Simon and Rachel entered the operations tent and Simon plopped into his desk chair, while Rachel perched herself on his desk top. He opened the message and read aloud for Rachel's benefit.

"From: His Eminence, Archbishop Charalampous, blah, blah, blah...To: Dr. Simon Cross, World's Greatest Archaeologist..."

Rachel smirked, "...and most full of himself!"

"Ok, I made that last part up, but it is, in fact, to me." Simon continued reading aloud, "We are in immediate need of your expertise at St. Onuphrius Monastery at Hakeldama, in the Valley of Hinnom. It appears we have stumbled on an archaeological find, which we believe to be an early Christian tomb of some significance. It would be greatly appreciated if you could assess the site as soon as possible. Please contact the monastery's Father Superior, Rev. Kamal Amman, at your earliest convenience and let him know if you are able to help. Respectfully, Archbishop Charalampous, blah, blah, blah."

"Blah, blah, blah is an odd sort of title for an archbishop," Rachel said playfully.

"Indeed." Simon laughed. "The Hinnom Valley," Simon sat back in his chair and placed his arms behind his head, "is a place with a rather dark history." He stared at the canvas ceiling thoughtfully.

"How so?" Rachel asked.

"Well, in ancient Jewish history, more than a thousand years before Christ, the people of Judah went against God and worshipped demons. They constructed an altar, called Topheth, in the Valley of Benhinnom (which means son of Hinnom) and, thereupon, they burned their children in sacrifice to the pagan god, Molech, and other demons. The Hebrew name for the valley is Ge Hinnom, which in Greek became Gehenna, the New Testament place of judgment and eternal fire. Hinnom became symbolically, and some might argue literally, Hell on earth."

Simon reached for his Bible and scanned through it, rapidly turning pages until he found what he was searching for. "Here it is...in Jeremiah 7, verses 31 through 33...*They have built the high places of Topheth, which is in the valley of the son of Hinnom, to burn their sons and their daughters in the fire, which I did not command, and it did not come into My mind.*

'Therefore, behold, days are coming,' declares the LORD, 'when it will no longer be called Topheth, or the valley of the son of Hinnom, but the valley of the Slaughter; for they will bury in Topheth because there is no other place. The dead bodies of this people will be food for the birds of the sky and for the beasts of the earth; and no one will frighten them away.'"

"Horrible," Rachel said, repulsed.

"Then," Simon explained, "the Jewish king, Josiah, went down into the valley and desecrated the altar so that it could no longer be used for such murderous practices. I think that's in *2nd Kings*, Chapter 23," Simon put his finger on the tab marked *2 Kings* and flipped the pages until he found the reference. "Yes, verse 10...*He, meaning Josiah, also defiled Topheth, which is in the valley of the son of Hinnom, that no man might make his son or his daughter pass through the fire for Molech.*"

"Good for Josiah!" Rachel commented.

"Indeed."

"So, what should we do about the Archbishop's tomb?"

"Well, it is intriguing, to say the least. And, we are making excellent progress here at Herodium. I say we pay the monastery a visit and see what they have unearthed."

"I'm in," Rachel said enthusiastically. "After the wedding, of course."

"Whatever it is, count me in too," a voice from the operations tent door spoke out.

Simon and Rachel looked up to see Jordan Goldberg standing in the door way. Jordan dropped his duffle bag on the floor with a thud.

"Jordan!" Rachel squealed. "You came for our wedding!"

"Wouldn't have missed it, especially after Moishe called early this morning."

"Glad to see you back, my young friend," Simon moved from his desk and hugged Jordan.

"Good to be back, Doctor."

"Have you had breakfast?" Rachel asked concernedly.

"Yes, but hours ago. Maybe some coffee?"

"Let's get you a cup before you get settled back in to your tent. Everything is right where you left it."

"Thank you, Doctor."

"Come, we'll fill you in on this newest opportunity for adventure!"

"Indeed," Jordan said in his best Simon Cross impersonation.

"Indeed," Simon said, feigning insult.

"He's got your number," Rachel laughed.

"Indeed," Simon repeated, even more indignantly.

chapter

NINE

For many deceivers have gone out into the world, those who do not acknowledge Jesus Christ as coming in the flesh. This is the deceiver and the antichrist.

Watch yourselves, that you do not lose what we have accomplished, but that you may receive a full reward.

- 2 John 1:7-8

HOUSTON, TEXAS.

Victoria "Missy" Morgan was still not used to being back stateside after her pilgrimage to Israel for *The Gathering*. As she made her way to her locker to unload her books before third lunch, she felt strange. It was as if she were just going through the motions of high school, conversations with friends, extra curricular activities and life at home. Nothing here gave her the same rush as her experiences in Israel. She was bored. Not the usual "there's nothing on TV and none of my friends are on Facebook" kind of bored, but deep, down-to-the-core bored.

Her friends had asked her about her prolonged absence from school. And, she had done her best to try and explain how she had felt compelled to go to Israel to answer God's call. But, many of them had not heard the call and didn't "get it," or maybe they had heard and had just ignored it out of ignorance or hard-heartedness. In Missy's experience, it was her own headstrong insistence that the family go, coupled with threats that she would find a way to go on her own, without them if necessary, that finally got her foster-mom, and her foster-mom's parents, to agree to pay for her, and her older brothers, to make the trip. Perhaps some of her friends didn't have the same resolve as she, to go at any cost. For whatever reason, she felt a sense of pity for them, a deep sadness, that they missed such a great opportunity to be truly blessed.

Now that she was home, her foster-family, especially her foster-mom, seemed completely disinterested in building on the foundation provided by her experience in Israel. Missy and her brothers had been in the foster home for so long, ever since their father's death, that she didn't even think of it as a foster home. She had really never known anything else. She fully expected them to embrace her enthusiasm for Christ, now that she had returned from Israel with the good news of the gospel.

"How is that even possible?" Missy wondered. "How could they witness the obvious enthusiasm and transformation in my life-view, from frivolous, materialistic teenager to thoughtful, spiritually-maturing Christian, all due to the miraculous events at *The Gathering,* and not want to get involved? How could anyone sit and listen to her tell of Father Proudman's amazing explanation about God's grace and mercy as poured out on mankind through the sacrifice of His own Son, and not be moved?"

Still, in Missy's house, she and her big brothers, C.P. and Alex, were the only ones who continued to grow in the faith. Her foster-mom, her foster-grandparents, everyone, but her brothers, was too self-absorbed. She wished her Dad were still alive. But, they had lost him, when she was only four, when American Airlines Flight 77 smashed into the Pentagon, where he worked in Naval Intelligence. He was a godly man. She had found and read his journals in the attic, and grew to know him through his own, beautifully written words. He would have led them and encouraged their new faith.

She had never known her mother, who had died from complications during her birth. All Missy knew of her mother was from pictures in dusty albums and from her older brother's foggy memories. C.P. was only three when she died, so they were more impressions than genuine memories.

Missy was just happy that C.P. could drive so that getting to their new church was not ever an issue. Even though she couldn't get the rest of the family to darken the door of a church, she, Alex and C.P. were there every Sunday, soaking up God's Word.

She especially loved youth group. She loved the worship music, and she loved sharing the highs and lows of her week with her youth group friends; but it was the Bible lessons and discussions that she loved most of all. There was something indescribably wonderful about learning of the people in the Bible, and of God's grace and love for His people. She loved being royalty; an heir to the kingdom; one of God's chosen, made worthy by Jesus Christ and his sacrifice on the cross.

As Missy sat down at the lunch table next to her best friend, Olivia, she realized that it was Wednesday, youth group day. "You are coming to youth group with me tonight, right bff?"

"Of course," Olivia said happily. "Ever since *The Gathering*, my parents have been very encouraging about it. And, they haven't missed a single Sunday! Mom is even singing on the worship team now! I mean, who knew she could sing, right?"

Missy laughed loudly, then grew suddenly serious. "I hear rumors that Pastor Jessie is leaving the church to start his own. Is that true?"

"That's what I heard too! OMG! And, I heard that he is trying to get people to go with him. He's splitting the church right down the middle! He's only been an associate pastor for a year or so. Does he really think he's ready to lead his own church? And, what about poor Pastor Shawn? He has to be feeling betrayed!"

"I don't like the whole thing," Missy said with a worried tone. "It seems to me that Christians shouldn't behave like Pastor Jessie, or those that are following him. I mean, I'm new to this whole church thing, but it doesn't take a lifelong church-goer to see that this thing stinks!"

"Well, I'm planning on bringing the whole thing up for discussion during youth group tonight. Inquiring minds want to know!"

"I know, right?" Missy responded.

Jessie Langer was tired of being associate pastor to Pastor Shawn. Although not an ordained minister, Jessie had taken on the job under Pastor Shawn so that he could learn and grow in preparation for ministry some day. He quickly lost sight of his place and mission and began to be self-absorbed and highly-critical of Pastor Shawn's leadership.

Jessie was outgoing and likeable on the surface. His boisterous personality matched his heavy-set frame. He was younger and more progressive than Shawn, so he developed closer ties to some of the younger members of the church, leading the men's group in poker night instead of Bible study, and developing an inappropriate relationship with a church member's wife when he was supposed to have been counseling them through a tough spot in their marriage.

Behind closed doors and at every opportunity, he began to drive a wedge between his followers and Pastor Shawn. During a two week vacation, Jessie attended a conference put on by *Tapestry,* an organization that helps those wanting to start new churches, and returned home fortified with false pride, self-admiration and ill-conceived ambition. He decided he was ready to start his own *Tapestry* plant church. He was delusional. He spent all of his time and a lot of the church's resources secretly creating a new website and printed materials for his new church, where the *"diversity of its members were like individual threads forming the beautiful tapestry of a community of faith."* Beautiful words, hollow in substance.

Jessie marched in to Pastor Shawn's office and told him that he was leaving the church and was taking many families with him. The news devastated Shawn on many levels. The church he had worked so hard to build was splitting, and he was heart-broken.

Pastor Shawn knew what had to be done. When Jessie showed up to lead youth group that night, Shawn met him at the door.

"You're not going to lead the kids tonight, Jessie."

"Why not?" Jessie said defiantly.

"Because I'm letting you go," Shawn said firmly. "You have undermined the peace and fabric of this church and you have not been honest with me or this congregation. Not to mention the fact that you misappropriated church property and performed non-church activities while on the church's time clock."

"Fine!" Jessie said angrily. "I'll just get my things."

"No. You'll have to wait until tomorrow. The kids are starting to show up and I'll not have you disrupting things and upsetting them before youth group."

"Whatever," Jessie said indignantly and turned to leave without further conflict. He walked to the parking lot, opened his car door and sat inside heavily, slamming the door behind him. He watched as youth group kids began to be dropped off in front of the church. Anger enveloped him like a suffocating blanket. He would show Pastor Shawn. His church would be huge and he would rub Shawn's nose in it at every opportunity.

As he fumed and sulked, the windows of his car began to fog. Then the fog became frost and Jessie realized he could see his breath. He wiped off the rearview mirror and froze in terror as he saw red, glowing eyes reflected back at him from the back seat.

"Did I startle you, Jessie?" The mouth below the eyes barely moved as it spoke in an unnervingly docile tone.

"Who are you?" Jessie whined.

"You know me, Jessie. You have always known me." The eyes and mouth began to materialize into a face. The skin was pale, almost translucent; the teeth were pointed and small, set behind thin gray lips. "I can help you get back at Pastor Shawn for his insolence. You can have your revenge. You can have a mega-church and laugh in his face at his paltry attempts to grow this little parish. All you have to do is help me get my revenge."

"What do I have to do?" Jessie's voice trembled.

"Listen carefully..."

ISRAEL. HERODIUM.

Simon Cross entered the maintenance tent to consult with Ali, the project's IT technician. Ali was busily running diagnostics on ISAIAH, the technological miracle that had been so instrumental in finding the scrolls hidden in the mikveh deep within Mt. Herod.

"Ali, just the man I want to see," Cross said exuberantly.

"Good afternoon, Dr. Cross. How are you today?"

"I'm well, Ali, thank you. And you?"

"I cannot complain, Doctor. The systems seem to be functioning quite reliably."

"Excellent, Ali. That's good to hear. We may need ISAIAH at another site in a few days."

"It will be ready, Doctor. You have my word."

"Your word is gold, Ali!"

"Thank you, Doctor. I do my best. So, Doctor," Ali changed the subject, "you are getting married tomorrow afternoon, yes?"

"Yes, indeed, Ali!"

"That is wonderful! Miss Rachel is such a fine lady! You are blessed, praise, Allah!"

"Yes, Ali, I am indeed! You are planning on attending, right?"

"Oh, yes, Doctor! I would not miss such a happy occasion. And, you and Miss Rachel have made me feel like one of the family. And, I'm sure that I will fit in with your religious ceremony well since we all worship the same God, yes?"

"Ali...I've been meaning to discuss that very idea with you for some time. Do you have time to talk?"

"I always have time for you, Doctor. What would you like to discuss, exactly?"

Simon Cross pulled a camp stool up to the work bench across from Ali, who sat patiently, waiting for Cross to begin the discussion. Simon put his finger to his lips contemplatively and then slowly and thoughtfully began to speak.

"Ali, I have tremendous respect for you and your work. More than that I feel that you and I are friends."

"Thank you, Doctor. I feel exactly the same."

Cross nodded and continued, "As you know, I have made the study of ancient civilizations, particularly those in the Holy Land, my life's work."

"Yes. You are a most respected expert in the field, Doctor. I know this to be true."

"So then, what I am about to share with you is based on archaeological evidence...understood?"

"Understood."

"The name of your god, Allah, is an ancient name, Ali, that predates Islam by thousands of years. Archaeologists, over the past century, have discovered evidence, in the form of inscriptions in numerous sites...Turkey, Syria, Persia and Egypt, just to name a few...which specifically refer to the Moon-god, *Sin*, who's title was *al ilah*, which means *the deity* or *the god*. This title did not mean 'only god' but, rather meant 'most important god' to the pagan Arabs of the time. The pagan deity, *Sin*, was one of many gods worshipped by pre-Islamic Arabs. His symbol was the crescent moon."

Simon Cross searched Ali's face to see if he was taking all of this in and to discern how it was being received.

"Many temples have been unearthed, including Mecca, dedicated to the Moon-god. And many carved idols, which bear his name, have been unearthed next to similar idols of other gods worshipped by polytheistic pagan Arabs. Over time, the pagans began to refer to *Sin* by his title, which eventually became Allah. In fact, all the evidence supports the idea that Allah is, in fact, the pagan Moon-god of pre-Islamic times. Mohammed's parents were Moon-god worshipers. This is historical fact. Mohammed grew up worshipping the Moon-god and several lesser deities. It was not until he created the concept of Islam that Mohammed banned the worship of the other gods in favor of Allah and monotheism. But, it was not so much a decision of faith in Allah as it was one of convenience and control. It was easier to dictate to one set of followers than to many diverse sets."

"Doctor, didn't Islam derive from Judaism and Christianity?"

"Alas, my friend, that is a concept that became popularized by later Islamic teaching seeking to lend credibility to the religion. Archaeological evidence proves otherwise. Additionally, the held over pagan traditions of Moon-god worship persist in Islam even today. For example, the crescent moon is the symbol of Islam, is it not? And isn't your traditional holy fast defined by the time between the appearances of the crescent moon in the night sky?"

"The answer to your questions is 'yes' Doctor. But, if Allah is not the God of the Bible, then who is?"

"Ali, the God of the Bible is Yahweh. He is the one true God. I am afraid that your Allah is nothing more than an idol, a made-up pagan deity perpetuated by Mohammed for political gain and power."

"This is a most distressing theory, Doctor. I am not sure what to make of it. I respect you and I trust that you are sincere, but this is a bit overwhelming all at once."

"I fully understand, Ali. And, it was not my desire to upset you, but I care enough about you that I am compelled to share with you what I know to be the truth."

"I will contemplate seriously what you have shared with me, Doctor. You must give me some time to process this and to investigate further for my own benefit."

"It pleases me that you are willing to consider it, Ali. Thank you for listening to me."

"After careful thought, I may have more questions than answers. May I count on you for continued discussion later, Doctor?"

"I would be honored, Ali. Whenever you are ready." Cross rose from the camp stool and patted Ali firmly on the shoulder as he exited the maintenance tent.

Ali sat staring into his computer screen with unseeing eyes. His mind was reeling and he felt lost, as if his spiritual compass had started spinning in the absence of any magnetic influence.

∞❦∞

Missy and Olivia were a bit surprised when Pastor Jessie was not leading the youth group that night. They knew he was leaving the church, but they had no idea it would be tonight. To their delight, the atmosphere seemed lighter and the music and worship time seemed even more meaningful.

"Wow, I feel really good about youth group tonight," Missy chattered excitedly to Olivia as they walked from the sanctuary to the front of the church. "It was so...alive tonight!"

"I know! I got much more out of it than, like...ever!" Olivia agreed.

The pair bounced energetically along and out the front door into the parking lot. Missy's eyes fixed on C.P.'s car under a street lamp and she grabbed Olivia's arm and pulled her in that direction. "C'mon, slowpoke!"

"I'll show you who's the slowpoke," Olivia broke free of Missy's grasp and bolted for the car. The two laughed as they raced, their attention so fixated on winning that they didn't notice Jessie sitting in his car right next to theirs. Still laughing, the girls playfully fought over the door handle, each trying to be the first one to the front seat.

"I've got shotgun!" Missy said.

"No, I called it!" Olivia responded knowing full well she hadn't actually called it.

"No you did not!" Missy protested.

"Well, I got here first!"

"Whatever!"

Missy continued to battle Olivia for the front seat, when suddenly she heard a crackle and Olivia dropped to the ground. Missy started to react when her body jolted and everything went black. As she lost consciousness, she thought she saw Pastor Jessie's reflection in the car window, holding a small lightning bolt and a syringe in his hands. In that split second, she also thought she saw a shadow next to him with eyes glowing red, as in a photograph taken with flash.

chapter

TEN

And I saw the holy city, new Jerusalem, coming down out of heaven from God, made ready as a bride adorned for her husband.

- Revelation 21:2

For Rachel, dawn broke over Herodium more beautifully than she had ever seen it. It was her wedding day. She sat on her cot and watched the sun rise, entranced by the magnificence of light and color. Where she thought there should have been butterflies in her stomach from nervousness, there were only warm feelings of peace and joy. Peace, from the knowledge that God's hand was on this marriage, and because she felt blessed at the idea of being the wife of a godly man like Simon. Joy, because she loved him immeasurably.

Rachel looked at the sparkling diamond on her finger. The early sun's rays streamed through the mesh tent window and intensified as they bounced around the facets of the stone. To Rachel's eyes, it seemed as if a miniature sun were rising on her hand. She smiled.

Her wedding would be special, she thought, not because of its extravagance, or pomp and circumstance, but because of its meaning. Rachel knew that she and Simon shared a love centered on Christ. She knew that the tremendous joy she felt was made possible by that Christ-centric focus. She would not have the most royal wedding gown ever, nor would her cake be like something out of a fairy tale. She would not arrive in a Rolls Royce or depart in a stretch-limo, and her reception would be in a mess tent at an archaeological dig instead of a country club's grand ballroom. But, all of that didn't matter to her, not even a little bit. Her wedding would be exceedingly special because the man she loved would be next to her; her best friends would be there to share in the moment; and her God would be present, not only at the wedding, but also in their marriage for the rest of their days.

Across the way, Simon Cross was wakening to the morning sun and to the happy realization that he was about to marry the beautiful Rachel Rosenkranz. He smiled as her image came to mind. What a special woman she was, he thought. Indeed, she would have to be an amazing woman to have softened Simon's heart in such a way. After losing his wife, Sarah, so many years ago, along with their baby, Cross thought, make that vowed, he would never find his way here again. But God was merciful and had other plans for Simon Cross. Rachel had entered his life with such incredible grace and beauty, that his heart seemed to thaw the instant he saw her.

Simon gazed blankly at the canvas roof over his cot. The cream-colored cloth had aged, with stains and water marks forming shapes and textures in the material. The shapes resembled animals and faces, in much the same fashion as do clouds when one looks at them with the open mind of imagination. With the morning sun lighting it from outside, the interior of his tent seemed to glow in a yellow-orange light. A pedestal fan oscillated, methodically pushing a cool breeze across his face intermittently. He basked in the hum and whoosh of the fan as it lulled him into a sleepy, half-awake trance.

From his sleepy state, thoughts of Sarah and of Rachel, drifted in and out of his mind in no specific pattern. Simon was as content as he had ever been. He began to pray.

"Father God, it's my wedding day and I owe it all to you. How blessed I am that you would, not once, but twice in my life, grant me incredible love and passion. What a generous and merciful God you are, Lord, that you pulled me out of deep tragedy and despair and gave me back my life, not just as good as it once was, but immeasurably, abundantly better than I have ever known. Thank you, Father. From the center of my heart, thank you for sending me Rachel."

The tranquility of the morning was abruptly broken as a caravan of vehicles, led by Moishe's Land Rover, rolled noisily into camp. The squeaking of brakes and the rough idle of diesel engines penetrated Simon's sleepy trance. Moishe's unmistakable accent, barking orders, brought a smile to Simon's face.

"Take the chairs to the top of Mt. Herod and set them up in the atrium as I showed you! Go!" Moishe directed a box lorry to the top of Mt. Herod with his emphatically pointing arm. "Joseph, the mess tent is over there. You will find everything you need. Where is my set-up crew? Let's move people, I want this mess tent looking like the Hilton's grand ballroom! We have a wedding to do in just hours! Move!"

Designers, decorators, caterers, and workers scurried in various directions. The beep, beep, beep of back-up warning alarms pierced the morning air as vehicles moved into position for unloading. Moishe's wedding task force had mobilized and nuptials were imminent.

Simon pulled on trousers and a khaki shirt and exited his tent into the bustling common area. He waved at Moishe, who grinned back at him. Rachel, too, exited her tent and joined Simon, amazed at the flurry of activity. "Oh, my," was all she could manage.

Moishe, seeing Rachel, stopped directing and trotted toward her. "My dear Rachel, I have something wonderful for you!" He motioned energetically at a white van that had only just entered the camp. The van rolled to a stop behind Moishe, and a somewhat flamboyant gentleman emerged from the passenger side, walked briskly around the front, and opened the sliding door facing Rachel and Simon. Hanging inside were four garment bags, two black, one white, one light blue.

"For the groom and best man, a handsome pair of matching tuxes," the tailor gestured like a model on a game show, "and for the lovely bride and her maid of honor, magnificent dresses, which I designed myself...if I may add!"

Simon chuckled. Rachel smiled and wiped a happy tear from under her right eye. Then, hugging Moishe tightly, she whispered, "Thank you, Moishe. Thank you, thank you, thank you."

"It was nothing, my dear one. Happy to do it."

"What was wrong with my usual khaki?" Simon kidded.

Rachel responded with a playful punch to Simon's shoulder. "Really, Simon?"

"Indeed."

"Right, then. Off you go with the tailor, Rachel. No time to waste. Must make sure it fits. Oh, and take this too...the beautiful bridesmaid's dress for the lovely Angelica." Moishe smiled as he loaded Rachel's arms to overflowing with the white and light blue garment bags and shoe boxes.

Rachel strained to kiss Simon over the pile of stuff in her arms and then waddled off to her tent with the tailor. Angelica emerged and rushed to Rachel's aid, removing several items from Rachel's arms before they fell to the ground. "Look what Moishe brought!" Rachel said excitedly. "There's even a bridesmaid's dress for you...and shoes!"

"There are shoes?" Angelica responded a little too enthusiastically. She glanced back at Moishe, "Oh, so you've discovered my weakness, Moishe? Not good..."

Moishe grinned and waved in response.

Simon swung the black garment bag across his shoulder and looked in Moishe's face. "My old friend, you have blessed me. You have made me, and the woman I love, very, very happy. Thank you, my friend."

As Moishe removed the second black garment bag from the van, he said, "Simon, my dear friend. Nothing gives me greater joy than to do this wedding for you and Rachel. I love you both dearly. Just rejoice in your day and leave everything to your old friend Moishe."

"Done."

"Excellent."

Missy Morgan regained consciousness. As she opened her eyes, fear gripped her completely. It was totally dark, very cold, and cramped. The floor was hard and rubberized and the walls that encapsulated her were made of a heavy wire mesh. She was caged. Her fuzzy mind then realized the sensation of movement and the uncomfortably loud rushing sound of jet engines. She was flying. She felt cautiously around her cramped cage and recoiled in horror when her fingers touched a human foot. "Who is that?" she said in a trembling voice. There was no response. Missy worked up her nerve and felt again, making contact with the foot a second time. She felt her way to the ankle and discovered a delicate chain anklet with a small cross-shaped charm. She knew instantly that it was Olivia. They both wore the same anklet as a symbol of their *bff* status.

"Olivia?" Missy found Olivia's face in the darkness and put her face close to Olivia's mouth, relieved to feel her friend exhale onto her cheek. She was warm to the touch. "Olivia, wake up." She stirred. "That's it, Olivia...wake up."

Olivia groaned and opened her eyes. "It's still dark out, Missy. Do we have to get up already? I'm cold. Did you take all the covers?"

"Olivia, we are <u>not</u> having a sleep over! Now wake up! This is serious!"

Olivia became more aware as Missy's tone sank in. "Where are we?"

"I don't know exactly, but we're in a cage...in an airplane. I think Pastor Jessie tazed us."

"Tazed? Pastor Jessie? Why?"

"I don't know, but there was...somebody...something... there with him."

"So, now what, Missy? I mean, how do we get out of here? What does he want with us? Is he crazy? Is he gonna hurt us?"

"I don't know, Olivia. All I know is we are gonna find a way out of this cage. Feel around your side and see if there's a door." Missy felt the sides of the cage, but could not discern by touch if there was any way to open it. "Anything on your side?"

"I can't tell," Olivia reported.

"Neither can I."

The girls huddled closer together for warmth and sat silently wondering how long they would be stuck in the darkness. Missy hugged her friend and the two of them prayed softly together, asking God for protection and deliverance from the terror of their captivity.

Geoffrey Proudman had slept through the morning's noise and activity. He had been up late working on his homily for the wedding. He wanted it to be perfect. After all, Simon and Rachel were dear to him, and they deserved his best effort. He was sure that he had given them just that by the time he had saved his work for the last time before shutting down his laptop.

Proudman noticed that the air in his tent had become warm and stagnant. As he opened one eye, he noticed that his fan was not working. He eyed the switch. It was in the on position. He followed the power cord from the fan's base to the outlet on the tent's center support. It was plugged in. "Hmpf," he grunted. No choice now but to roll out of the rack. Sleeping would no longer be an option as the tent became a sweat box. He sat up and rubbed his eyes. He reached for the water bottle by his cot and was dismayed to find it empty. "Mess tent," he grumbled.

Geoffrey pulled on his trousers and t-shirt, shoved his feet into a pair of Nike's and made his way across the common area to the mess tent. Opening the screen door, he was somewhat disoriented as the interior of the tent was not the drab, utilitarian facility he knew. Round tables with white linens had replaced the long tables with benches. Flowers and candelabra center pieces replaced the condiment trays in the table centers. The ceiling and walls were adorned with translucent white cloth and white Christmas lights nestled within the cloth gave the room a magical glow.

"Wow." Geoffrey said out loud.

"My thought exactly," Jordan Goldberg chimed in from the coffee dispenser.

"Jordan...great to see you. What an amazing transformation the mess tent has had, eh?"

"Yes, that's an understatement. So are you ready to marry these two off?"

"Yes, I think so. I was up late finishing up the service, so I'm a little behind the power curve this morning."

"That makes two of us. I haven't slept well in ages. Keep having nightmares about Miriam."

"Sorry to hear that, Jordan. Maybe we can visit later and talk about things...after the wedding. If, you want, that is."

"Maybe. I mean, sure, I guess. I don't know."

"Well, just let me know. I'm here whenever you are up to it. No pressure."

"Thanks. Coffee?"

"No thanks. I just really need some water. The fan in my room went out at some point and I must have sweated out all of my reserves."

"Oh, you are more than likely a victim of Moishe's wedding extravaganza. They've commandeered all available outlets to power the light show you see before you," Jordan motioned toward the tent's glowing ceiling and walls.

"Makes sense. Guess I better get it in gear. Just a few hours now until go-time. See ya later?"

"Yeah, see ya." Jordan turned his attention back to preparing his coffee.

Geoffrey grabbed a bottle of water from the cooler and headed back across to his tent. "Shower and then one more look at the sermon," he said to himself. He walked back with a little more bounce in his step on the return trip. "This is the day that the Lord has made," he said to himself, "and, what a glorious day it is, too!"

Inside Rachel's tent, the tailor was busily sticking pins in the fabric of Rachel's wedding gown as she was perched atop a wooden cable spool turned on its side like a pedestal.

"Oh my, someone's fabulous," the tailor would say in a sing-song voice, which would cause both Rachel and Angelica to laugh uncontrollably. "Ok, silly, hold still or I might stick you with one of these pins, accidentally, of course."

"You look beautiful," Angelica said matter-of-factly. "What a gorgeous dress."

"Thank you," the tailor responded before Rachel had the opportunity. "I designed this, just for you, at Mo's request."

"Mo?" Rachel mouthed to Angelica, who stifled her gut reaction to fall over laughing.

"Well, you out did yourself," Angelica managed. "It truly is beautiful."

"A beautiful gown for a beautiful girl," the tailor said, hands on his hips, eyeing Rachel in the gown. "Ok, so out of the dress, girlfriend, so I can do some sewing where these pins are. Hurry, hurry...no time to waste!"

"Angie, can you unzip me, please?"

"Sure, come down off of there so I can reach," Angelica helped Rachel off of the pedestal and slid the zipper down with a long, smooth motion.

Rachel slipped out of the gown and handed it to the tailor, who bunched it carefully and swished out of the tent in a flurry. Rachel reached for her robe and sat on the cable spool where she had just been standing. "You simply have to try on that bridesmaid's dress."

"Oh, yes. Help me?"

"Yep."

Angelica unzipped the light blue garment bag and removed an elegant light blue dress; simple in design and mid-thigh in length. "Oh, my, it's gorgeous."

"It is gorgeous," Rachel agreed. Moishe has such good taste.

"You mean, Mo, don't you?" Both women laughed hysterically.

"So, try it on," Rachel urged.

Angelica slipped out of her shorts and t-shirt and stepped gingerly into the dress, one long, slender leg at a time. "Zip me?"

Rachel zipped and stood back to assess Angelica. The dress fit Angelica's body like a glove, conforming to her curves and accentuating the length of her shapely frame. "Wow! You can't wear that!"

"Why? What's wrong with it?"

"You'll completely steal the show!"

"Yeah, right."

"Seriously, You look...fabulous!" Rachel did her best to imitate the tailor's sing-song voice, placing one hand on her hip and the other to her cheek. The two shared yet another hysterical laugh. They were becoming great friends.

"The shoes!" Angelica blurted out suddenly. "Must see the shoes!"

Rachel opened a shoe box. "Nope. Those are white satin and adorable. Must be mine." She opened the second box, revealing a matching pair of light-blue heels. "Equally adorable!" Rachel dangled them in front of her by their thin straps.

"Indeed." Angelica tried to imitate Simon.

"No, you have to look more stoic and serious," Rachel corrected her.

"Indeed," Angelica tried again, furrowing her brow and lowering her voice even deeper.

"That's it!" Rachel laughed.

"So, gimme the shoes." Angelica pointed her painted toes and slipped into the shoes that Rachel placed in front of her on the pedestal. Rachel fastened the delicate straps around her ankles and stood back.

"Ok. That does it. You're wearing jeans and sneakers."

"What?" Angelica protested. She stood on the pedestal, dress and shoes accenting the excellent thoroughbred shape that God had given her.

"Sister," Rachel said softly. "You look amazing. Wait until Geoffrey Proudman gets a look at you. We may have to do a double wedding."

Angelica blushed. "I don't know about all of that. But, I hope he likes it."

"Girl, if he doesn't like it, I'm gonna fix him up with the tailor!"

Angelica dissolved in laughter. Rachel followed suit. Their laughter drifted through the camp, causing smiles to break out everywhere it touched an ear.

Geoffrey Proudman stood motionless in the shower, letting the hot water melt the tension from his neck and shoulders. His wedding homily ran through his mind, and he paused now and then to try different words and phrasing. While this homily was especially meaningful to him, the mental exercise was something he did with all of his sermons, and not unique to this specific situation. It was not that he wanted his delivery to be rehearsed, but rather that he wanted to know what he intended to say backwards and forwards, so that when he did it for real, he would be even more receptive to the leading of the Holy Spirit. There were many times when the sermon he delivered ended up being far different from what was originally conceived due to the Spirit moving him in one direction or another. Proudman loved it when that happened, because the result was always much more impactful than his original version.

Geoffrey turned off the water somewhat reluctantly and stepped onto the wooden slats of the shower tent floor. He dried and dressed quickly, anxious to spend some quiet time preparing on the mountain top. He grabbed his backpack, his walking stick, and on the way across camp, ducked into his tent for a moment to retrieve his Native American flute. When Proudman truly needed to get to a more prayerful place, he almost always picked up his flute. There was something calming and spiritually satisfying about its warm, full tones.

Upon reaching the top of Mt. Herod, Proudman perched himself on one of the crumbling stone walls around Herodium's perimeter. He looked down at Lower Herodium and saw the *Radiant UMC* mission team's camp. He looked across to the University's base camp and felt peacefully removed from the hustle and bustle of the wedding preparations. Down in the atrium of Herodium, the set-up crew had finished placing chairs in neat rows facing the ramp and altar where Simon and Rachel would say their vows in just a couple more hours. Tall candelabras, one per step, lined each side of the ramp, which Rachel would walk down to join Simon. More candelabras lined the atrium's perimeter where the audience would sit. Proudman could only imagine how incredibly beautiful the scene would look once the candles were lit and the sun settled below the horizon.

He reached for his flute and began to play his favorite Blackfoot melody. It was, appropriately enough, a romantic courting song passed down through generations of Blackfoot tribesmen. It also, conveniently, made for a perfect meditation song, with its soft, melodious tones, gentle runs and soulful tremolos. Proudman played. The notes carried into the late afternoon and Proudman drifted with them. As he played, he prayed. "Father, empty me. Use me to do your will in joining Simon and Rachel. Let me speak as if I am speaking the very words of God. Let me glorify you. Let this wedding, and this life-long marriage, be for your glory. Keep me humble and create in me a pure heart. Let me live for you. I pray in the mighty name of Jesus. Amen." As the last word of prayer concluded in his thoughts, the last sustained note from his flute floated away with the wind, as if lifting his prayer heavenward. Proudman felt satisfied. He picked up his things and set off for the base camp to get dressed for the wedding.

The frigid temperature and the constant droning of the aircraft's engines were taking their toll on Missy and Olivia. The ominous darkness and uncertain future struck chords of fear in the two teenagers the likes of which they had never known. For long hours, they drifted in and out of semi-sleep, frequently jolting into hyper-alertness due to anxious apprehension.

After what seemed like an eternal purgatory, there was a noticeable change in the sound of the engines, and the whirr and thump of mechanical movement and hydraulics could be heard with absolute clarity from their location in the aircraft's hold. The landing gear deployed and locked and within minutes, the familiar chirp of the rubber wheels touching down on the runway gave the girls a new sense of terror. They wondered what was in store for them in whatever place they had just landed.

As the girls steeled themselves against what might come next, the unmistakable sound of a cell phone ringing on top of the cage caught them completely off guard. After three distinct rings, an aerosol spray blasted into the cage filling it with a noxious odor. The girls had just enough time to scream, once each, before the spray caused them to fight desperately for breath; and, one after the other, their tear-filled eyes closed as they fell limp in a heap in the center of the cage, mouths agape, gasping for air.

The hour had finally come. The Reverend Geoffrey Proudman, in his priestly robes, made his way to Simon's tent. There he found Simon and Moishe looking like 007 in their tailored tuxes.

"Any priestly advice, Padre?" Simon said as Proudman entered the tent.

"Yes, as a matter of fact," Geoffrey responded. "Marry her quickly before she changes her mind!"

"Well, let's get on with it then," Simon laughed.

Moishe held the tent's screen door open. "This way to your limo, sir."

The trio exited and climbed into Moishe's Land Rover for the short trip to the summit of Mt. Herod. Guests from the University and Jerusalem were already being shuttled up the mountain and were being seated in Herodium's atrium.

"I hadn't really expected so many people to show on such short notice. And we didn't send formal invitations," Simon admitted as they drove upward.

"I've been busy," Moishe shrugged. "I made some calls. What are you going to do? You have a wedding...you should have people to watch."

"Indeed."

Moishe parked the Land Rover and the men walked up to the edge of the ramp leading down to the large stone altar. Below the altar, the guests were looking up at them from the floor of the atrium. The candles around the floor, and on the tiered ramp, were being lit as the sun began its descent. The sky above the open atrium began to display an incredible array of colors: reds, oranges, purples and golds mixed like watercolors. God was creating a glorious setting for the ceremony about to unfold.

A string quartet began to play softly, adding to the ambiance as Simon, Moishe and Geoffrey took their places on the altar at the base of the ramp. They looked back up the ramp expectantly, waiting for the maid of honor and the bride to appear at the top. Simon occupied himself by looking at the faces in the audience and waving to those he knew who caught his eye.

It was only a matter of minutes before Angelica's radiance appeared at the top of the ramp. On cue, the music changed and she began her slow descent toward the altar. The audience was mesmerized as she walked. Her long, dark, satin hair swished gently from side to side behind her as she moved to the music's tempo, her graceful form captivating everyone below; and Geoffrey Proudman most of all. He felt his pulse increase and his breath shorten. "How incredibly beautiful she is," he thought.

Simon leaned toward him and said lowly, "Steady there, Padre."

"Hot," Geoffrey muttered back to Simon, "it's suddenly very hot in these robes."

Simon and Moishe eyed each other knowingly and chuckled. Geoffrey watched Angelica all the way to her position on the altar opposite Moishe. He smiled sheepishly at her when she stopped and leaned into her ear, whispering, "You are breathtaking." Angelica kissed his cheek softly and smiled at him as he moved back to his spot on the altar.

The music changed and all eyes looked to the top of the ramp. Rachel appeared and paused for a moment, taking in the magnificent scene. The ancient ruins were bathed in the soft golden light of the nearly extinguished sun. The sky was full of wispy clouds that soaked up the hues of red, orange and purple. The rows of candles lining the ramp and around the perimeter of the atrium were beginning to glow in the shadows that overtook the surrendering light. In her most vivid imagination, she could not have created a more perfect backdrop for her wedding. She felt blessed.

From Simon's perspective, an angel had appeared on the edge of Herodium. Her gown, like the wispy clouds above, soaked up the colors of the setting sun and the golden glow of the fading light shimmered off of her hair like a halo. Simon felt his heart skip beats and he could not help but smile widely.

Geoffrey leaned in and returned the favor, "Steady there, Doc."

Simon nodded in agreement. "You're right, Padre. It has gotten hot down here."

Geoffrey nodded. Moishe chuckled. Angelica rolled her eyes playfully.

Jordan Goldberg moved in beside Rachel and offered his arm in escort. Rachel began the descent on Jordan's arm. Her gown fit snugly, showing off her slender form. Her bare, tan shoulders looked golden in the candle light and her face radiated joy as her eyes met Simon's. She glided into place and stood looking up into Simon's face as Jordan descended the five steps on the right side of the altar and took his seat in the atrium.

"I'm breathless," Simon whispered to her, "you look... amazing."

Rachel simply smiled appreciatively in response. The couple faced Proudman and the ceremony began as the priest held his hands in blessing over all present and prayed, *"Father God, who has filled the world with beauty: Open our eyes to behold your gracious hand in all your works; that, rejoicing in your whole creation, we may learn to serve you with gladness; for the sake of him through whom all things were made, your Son Jesus Christ our Lord. Amen."*

Geoffrey smiled at Simon, and then at Rachel, and began the marriage liturgy, *"Dearly beloved: We have come together in the presence of God to witness and bless the joining together of this man and this woman in Holy Matrimony. The bond and covenant of marriage was established by God in creation, and our Lord Jesus Christ adorned this manner of life by his presence and first miracle at a wedding in Cana of Galilee. It signifies to us the mystery of the union between Christ and his Church, and Holy Scripture commends it to be honored among all people.*

The union of husband and wife in heart, body, and mind is intended by God for their mutual joy; for the help and comfort given one another in prosperity and adversity; and, when it is God's will, for the procreation of children and their nurture in the knowledge and love of the Lord. Therefore marriage is not to be entered into unadvisedly or lightly, but reverently, deliberately, and in accordance with the purposes for which it was instituted by God."

Geoffrey addressed the congregation seated in the atrium below, *"Into this holy union Simon and Rachel now come to be joined. If any of you can show just cause why they may not lawfully be married, speak now; or else for ever hold your peace."* No one moved.

The priest then spoke with authority directly to Simon and Rachel, *"I require and charge you both, here in the presence of God, that if either of you know any reason why you may not be united in marriage lawfully, and in accordance with God's Word, you do now confess it."*

After a moment's pause, Geoffrey turned to Rachel and asked, *"Rachel, will you have this man to be your husband; to live together in the covenant of marriage? Will you love him, comfort him, honor and keep him, in sickness and in health; and, forsaking all others, be faithful to him as long as you both shall live?"*

Rachel looked into Simon's eyes. She could see her joy in them reflected back at her. She wanted nothing more than to be with him for the rest of her days. "I will," she said softly.

Geoffrey turned to his friend, Simon, and repeated the question, *"Simon, will you have this woman to be your wife; to live together in the covenant of marriage? Will you love her, comfort her, honor and keep her, in sickness and in health; and, forsaking all others, be faithful to her as long as you both shall live?"*

Simon felt at peace. Everything he had ever loved about Rachel seemed to well up within him. There was nothing he would rather do than proclaim his intentions, here on this mountain top, in front of God and all of his friends and colleagues. "I will," he said intently.

Geoffrey then looked out to the congregation, and held his arms out as if to embrace them all, and asked, *"Will all of you witnessing these promises do all in your power to uphold these two persons in their marriage?"*

Completely enchanted by the moment, the congregation, gathered below the altar, answered in unison, "We will."

Missy could hear groaning. It woke her from her unconscious state and caused her to open her eyes to the realization that the groans were coming from her own mouth.

Her head pounded and she could taste the remnants of the noxious chemical that rendered her unconscious as the airplane landed. She could feel the cold, hard, stone floor beneath her. As her vision came into focus, she could see that the ceiling and walls were stone also. She tried to change positions, but as she did, the motion of her right leg was abruptly halted by a chain shackled to her ankle. The chain ran along the floor and attached to a ring embedded in the stone wall. Her left leg was free, as were her hands.

She sat up cautiously, very aware of her throbbing head. She turned to survey her prison and saw Olivia chained in the same manner to the opposite wall. They were in the same cell, although the chains would prevent them from huddling together and offering one another comfort as they had done in the cage on the plane.

"Olivia," Missy whispered. "Olivia," she said again more insistently. Olivia stirred and moaned reaching for her head. "Olivia, wake up."

"Oooh, not again. Why does this keep happening to me?"

"Olivia, look at me."

She looked.

"We're in a cell somewhere. Your leg is chained to the wall, but I think we both have enough chain so that I can at least touch your hand. Try."

Olivia slowly sat up, rubbing her temples and groaning again. "Ouch."

"C'mon try."

Olivia scooted across the hard floor and stretched out toward Missy, who did the same. When on their stomachs with arms stretched out, they could grasp hands. Just the ability to touch provided them with a small measure of re-assurance. Now, at least, they could hold hands and pray together.

"Why are they doing this to us?" Olivia tried to sup-press the fear and the tears, but failed on both counts.

"I don't know why. And I don't even know who 'they' are, except I think that Pastor Jessie has something to do with it. And, I think we are a long way from home; we were on that plane for hours."

As the girls clasped hands for comfort, the sound of a heavy door creaking on the other side of their iron cell door sent chills up their backs. Then, the clanking of keys against the cell door raised goose bumps on their skin. Mis-sy's mind raced with images of every horror movie she had ever seen and she squeezed Olivia's hands, bracing herself to release a blood curling scream at whatever ghastly thing appeared from behind the cell door. As the lock clanked open and the door squealed on its hinges, Olivia closed her eyes as if that action would hide her in some way from the horror, which had to be coming next.

Pastor Jessie's pasty white face poked around the edge of the door. He entered the cell carrying a jug of water, sandwiches and a bucket. "Here. I brought you something to eat and some water."

"What are you going to do with us?" Olivia asked cautiously, not really wanting to hear the answer.

"What's the bucket for?" Missy asked with attitude.

Jessie chose to address Missy's question. "Well, in case you haven't noticed, there's no toilet in here."

"That's gross," Missy protested. "Can we at least have some toilet paper?"

"I'll see what I can do," Jessie replied unconcernedly.

"So now what?" Missy asked defiantly. "You can't keep us locked up here forever, you know."

"I can do whatever I please," Jessie growled back. "So I'd watch my tone and attitude if I were you, girlie. Bad things might happen to you if you make me angry."

"Yeah, well you just wait until my brothers come for us," Missy tried to keep a brave front.

"Good luck with finding you," Jessie laughed. "By the time this is all over, everyone you know will be gone, and you...well, let's just say that there is something special in store for you and your priest friend."

"Priest friend? Father Proudman? What's he got to do with this? Do you have him in a cell? Is he alright? What have you done, Jessie? What happened to you? You're supposed to be a pastor. What's your problem?"

"Enough! Shut your yap, girlie!" Jessie grabbed Missy's face in his sweaty, pudgy hands and lifted her up by her head. She kicked her unchained leg at him and pounded him with her fists until he dropped her back to the hard floor. He then exited hastily. Clearly agitated, he slammed the cell door, and the one on the other side of it in kind, on his way out.

Missy waited until she was sure he was gone before dissolving in sobs and tears. She curled into a ball on the stone floor. Olivia tried to reach her to console her, but all she could do was stretch and strain against the chain that bound her to the wall. Olivia cried too. There was nothing else she could do.

Geoffrey Proudman closed his eyes for a moment and felt a peace come over him. He surrendered his ego and his will, and the Holy Spirit engulfed him. "Let your Word flow through me, Father," he said quietly. As he opened his eyes again, he began his homily.

"I don't have to tell most of you gathered here this evening, to witness this sacred event, what amazing, wonderful people are Simon and Rachel. Most of you know them as colleagues and friends; so you know already the solid content of their character. What you may not be aware of is the incredible depth of their faith, their passionate love for each other, and their love for their Lord, Jesus Christ.

I'm sure those of you of Christian faith have heard that a Christian wedding is symbolic of the relationship between Christ and His church; Christ being the bridegroom; and the church, the body of believers, being the bride. For those of you familiar with the *Old Testament*, this is the same relationship as found in the *Book of Isaiah, Chapter 62, verse 5:* *'For as a young man marries a virgin, So your sons will marry you; And as the bridegroom rejoices over the bride, So your God will rejoice over you.'*

This Truth is important, especially to Simon and Rachel, as they enter into these vows because it sets the tone for their human union to be based on and in something bigger and more wonderful than themselves. Their marriage is a holy relationship, not just between the two of them, but between them and God. Why is this distinction so vitally important? It is of primary importance because the very acknowledgement of God, through the intercessory power of Christ, as the epicenter of their marriage, guarantees its purity, its holiness, its longevity...its success. How is that possible, you ask? How is a successful marriage guaranteed? The answer is, as with many of God's Truths, astonishingly simple. As Simon and Rachel live out the days of their marriage with their eyes ever focused on Christ at the center of their union; then, all decisions affecting the marriage, all attitudes brought into the marriage home, all aspects of their individual lives, pass through the filters of Divine Mind and Divine Love and their influence over them as children of God.

What are the effects of such filters? The removal of impurities: The removal of selfish decisions; the tempering of bad attitudes; the purification of motives; intentions and things that crush the success of many human unions, embarked upon without the inclusion of God in the midst of them.

So, you are witnessing an event of Divine Love. A passionate affair of the heart, to be sure; but one based on something much deeper, more resilient, more eternal, more spiritual than just love on a human scale. Make no mistake... God is present here. The Holy Spirit has descended on this mountain and marked this couple as God's own forever. And in the mighty name of Jesus, I claim royal blessings for Simon and Rachel and for their marriage. *Amen.*"

Jessie Langer, his nose bleeding from the pounding that Missy had dealt him, sulked his way up the dark steps underneath St. Onuphrius and into Father Kamal Amman's office. Abaddon had resumed his guise as Kamal, and was ready to implement the next phase of his revenge. "So when do I get my mega-church," Jessie said as he slumped heavily into a chair across from Kamal's desk and wiped his bloody nose on his sleeve. "I did exactly what you asked. I got the Morgan girl here and her friend as a bonus. So, I'd like what's coming to me...now."

Abaddon was amused by Langer's insistence. "You really are delightfully evil for a pastor. Patience. You'll get what's coming to you in my good time. I need you to focus on keeping the little Christians alive for a while longer, feeding them and so forth, until I have Proudman and Cross and the rest of those insolent pests under the crushing weight of my revenge. Understood?"

"I guess so. They are so annoying though. And, they fight like cornered cats." Jessie wiped his nose again. "They've always been a pain in my backside. Little, pretty, popular girls, with personalities, and friends. I just want to hurt them in so many ways."

"You'll have the opportunity soon enough. But for now, they continue to breathe, yes?"

"Ok." Jessie pushed himself to his feet slothfully and turned to leave the office.

"Oh and one more thing, Jessie..." Abaddon rose from his chair and pierced Jessie's soul with fiery red eyes, "if you ever use that insolent, demanding tone with me again, I will feed your fat, disgusting body to the dogs, one piece at a time, while you are still breathing. Am I clear?"

"Clear." Jessie said weakly, wetting himself as he responded. He retreated to the hallway and ran to his room to change.

Father Proudman opened his *Bible* and, projecting out into the congregation with a strong voice, said, "The Holy Gospel of our Lord Jesus Christ according to Saint John: *'As the Father loved Me, I also have loved you; abide in My love. If you keep My commandments, you will abide in My love, just as I have kept My Father's commandments and abide in His love. These things I have spoken to you, that My joy may remain in you, and that your joy may be full. This is My commandment, that you love one another as I have loved you.'* The Gospel of the Lord."

Those in the congregation familiar with the custom responded, "Praise to you, Lord Christ."

Proudman nodded to Simon, who took Rachel's hand in his and looked into her face. His heart was full, and she was so absolutely perfect, standing there looking back at him. He smiled and said, "In the Name of God, I, Simon, take you, Rachel, to be my wife, to have and to hold from this day forward, for better for worse, for richer for poorer, in sickness and in health, to love and to cherish, until we are parted by death. This is my solemn vow."

Rachel, in kind, took Simon's hand in hers. She had thought about this moment many times, but there was no imaginary scene that she had ever played out in her head that compared to this actual moment. "In the Name of God, I, Rachel, take you, Simon, to be my husband, to have and to hold from this day forward, for better for worse, for richer for poorer, in sickness and in health, to love and to cherish, until we are parted by death. This is my solemn vow."

Proudman nodded to Moishe and then to Angelica, who stepped toward the priest and placed the rings into his waiting hand. With the rings in his left hand and his right hand raised heavenward, he prayed, "Bless, O Lord, *these rings* to be *a sign* of the vows by which this man and this woman have bound themselves to each other; through Jesus Christ our Lord. *Amen.*"

Simon took the smaller band from the priest's hand and gently pushed the wedding ring on to his bride's trembling finger saying, "Rachel, I give you this ring as a symbol of my vow, and with all that I am, and all that I have, I honor you, in the Name of the Father, and of the Son, and of the Holy Spirit." Simon was taken with the holiness of the moment. To realize that the ring he had just placed on Rachel's finger was a tangible, outward sign of an inward, spiritual promise made to her by him, in accordance with the will of the Father.

Rachel then took the other band from the priest's hand and placed it on Simon's finger and reciprocated, "Simon, I give you this ring as a symbol of my vow, and with all that I am, and all that I have, I honor you, in the Name of the Father, and of the Son, and of the Holy Spirit." Rachel wept.

She had come so far in her walk of faith. To think that a few short months ago, she had no idea that grace existed. And, now, she was experiencing the love of God poured out on her in this moment in the form of a blessed vow made to her by the man she loved so deeply.

Proudman then took Simon's right hand and joined it to Rachel's right hand. He placed both of his hands on theirs and looked beyond them to the congregation, who sat, smiling, below the altar. Proudman was full of joy for his friends; and he knew in his core that this marriage glorified God. And, he was relieved, somewhat, by the knowledge that this promise he made to Simon and Rachel had been fulfilled. He had married them. Mission accomplished. He grinned widely and announced, "Now that Simon and Rachel have given themselves to each other by solemn vows, with the joining of hands and the giving and receiving of a ring, I pronounce that they are husband and wife, in the Name of the Father, and of the Son, and of the Holy Spirit. Those whom God has joined together let no one put asunder."

The congregation resounded heartily, "Amen," and broke into tremendous applause for the newlyweds. Simon and Rachel waved from the altar.

"And now," Proudman held his hands up to still the crowd. "And now, Simon, you may kiss your bride!" The crowd resumed their applause as Simon leaned into Rachel, who responded by rising on her toes to meet him.

Simon and Rachel kissed for mere moments, but in that simple embrace, which symbolically sealed their union, they were lost in each other forever. As their lips touched, God smiled.

Moishe moved in and wrapped his big arms around the couple. Geoffrey stood next to Angelica, who took his arm and kissed his cheek gently. They watched the happy couple leave Moishe's bear hug and walk, hand-in-hand, up the ramp to a waiting car. At that point, Moishe turned to the crowd and announced, "Dr. and Mrs. Simon Cross cordially invite you to celebrate their union at a reception immediately following in the camp site below. Please come and enjoy!"

"Well, that's done," Geoffrey sighed to Angelica.

"You did a beautiful job. It was an amazing wedding, Geoffrey."

"It was, wasn't it?" Geoffrey agreed. "Let's hit that reception, shall we? I'm famished!"

"Right beside you, Padre. Right beside you."

chapter

ELEVEN

But God, being rich in mercy, because of His great love with which He loved us,

even when we were dead in our transgressions, made us alive together with Christ (by grace you have been saved),

and raised us up with Him, and seated us with Him in the heavenly places in Christ Jesus,

so that in the ages to come He might show the surpassing riches of His grace in kindness toward us in Christ Jesus.

- Ephesians 2:4-7

Proudman had retired early from the festivities at Simon and Rachel's wedding reception. It wasn't that he was not enjoying the unparalleled feast, which Moishe had orchestrated; on the contrary, he and Angelica had danced into the evening and there was not a single memory of the occasion that failed to bring a smile to his lips. It was by all accounts perfect. Still, when Angelica began to fade and yawn politely behind her hand, he had asked her if she wanted to turn in. She nodded to him with a sleepy smile in her eyes, so he walked her to her tent. It was there, at her door, that she planted a most incredibly passionate kiss on him before slipping from his grasp into the darkness of her dwelling. Every fiber of Proudman's being prickled with desire, but he dared not follow her inside, lest they embark on a path far askew to the straight and narrow one.

As he walked happily from her tent, thanking God for the strength to stay true to his ultimate intentions with Angelica, he decided that the sanctuary of his cot would be the best place for him. Besides, he reasoned, after the kiss Angelica had just given him, anything else the celebration in the mess tent had to offer would certainly be anticlimactic. He plopped down on his cot heavily. The moment his head hit the pillow and the cool breeze of his fan whooshed across his face, he felt the last of his energy leave him. Not even the music and laughter from the mess tent across the way would keep his eyes from closing. Proudman slept.

Perhaps it was the level of exhaustion from such an intensely spiritual day, or perhaps it was the third glass of Moishe's ridiculously expensive champagne, but Geoffrey

Proudman, in his slumber, returned to days past as he had done on many excruciating nights before; reliving the horrors of his former warrior life.

Lieutenant Proudman sat in a puddle of his own sweat. The MOPP suit protecting him, at least for now, from the lewisite blister agent on the outside would soon be his demise from within. The temperature inside his protective suit was easily 130 degrees and dehydration was occurring rapidly. To make matters worse, there was no effective way to disinfect his gas mask's drinking tube or its connection to his canteen, making the probability of ingesting some of the deadly chemical very high should he choose to attempt to drink.

The fact that he was not alone in his misery was even more concerning to him. Already three of his Marines had succumbed to the heat and were experiencing heat exhaustion. They were just minutes away from full on heat stroke and death, but there was nothing to be done; removing the suit to cool them down or administer fluids would kill them by inhalation or ingestion of the deadly dew.

If he and his men were to survive this chemical attack, they would need decontamination immediately. Proudman radioed his battalion CP with an NBC-1 report, which set into motion a frenzy of activity from battalion to regiment to division. A chemical attack was unprecedented in this war. The Iraqis didn't have chemical weapons of mass destruction according to the war's detractors, but from Proudman's sweaty perspective, the Iraqis had at least enough to make his life a living hell.

Proudman didn't take much encouragement from battalion's response to "hang in there" so he began to systematically assess his men. He moved around the perimeter to each fighting hole and checked each man's condition. The heat stress was taking its toll. Three down hard to heat stroke; one case of heat exhaustion; and the rest of the advance party was generally irritated with the enemy. As he moved as quickly as possible in the sweat soaked MOPP suit, he surmised that the sweat was significantly shortening the effective time of the suit. The charcoal lining was losing its ability to absorb the blister agent and it wouldn't be long before the chemical would completely compromise the suit. The only question was, which would kill them first; heat and dehydration, or lewisite poisoning?

Lieutenant Proudman was particularly concerned for the greener Marines. One in particular was showing signs of mental duress: PFC Cameron. "How're you doing, Cameron?" Proudman asked.

"When are they comin' to decon us, sir? I can't take this no more. I gotta get outta this suit."

"They're coming, Cameron. You sit tight and do not remove so much as a glove of that suit! You get me, Marine?"

"Aye, sir."

Proudman moved off to the next fighting hole just as mortar rounds began exploding within their position. Hell had just gone downhill. Somewhere in the chaos, energized by the exploding mortar shells, PFC Cameron reached his breaking point. From his position, Proudman could see an unmasked Marine running from his fighting hole, exposed to the white-hot shrapnel of the enemy's barrage. He didn't get very far, but it was not the mortars that put him down. Proudman ran from his fighting hole into the dust and smoke and fire, reaching PFC Cameron in seconds.

"Where's your mask, Marine!" Cameron's gas mask was no where around, not that it would have done him any good at this point. Cameron's throat, lungs and eyes were becoming goo. He gurgled and coughed as the blister agent did its work. Proudman could only cradle Cameron's head and firmly squeeze his hand as he passed. Proudman barely noticed the jets, which screamed in from out of nowhere, unloading their ordinance on a distant enemy position. The mortars stopped. Moments later, the decontamination vehicle rolled into the position. Relief for everyone but PFC Cameron.

Proudman woke with a start; the image of PFC Cameron's blistered eyes and face still burned into his mind. It was always the faces of the dead that haunted his sleep. Their lifeless eyes looked at him accusingly, making him question his faith, his ability to be redeemed, his worthiness to be forgiven, his very salvation...Every time the faces tormented him, he would go to God in prayer, claiming the redeeming blood of Jesus Christ as his saving grace. Proudman knew that without Christ, his soul would surely be lost.

A few miles away, in Kamal's chambers at Hakeldama, a delighted Abaddon reveled in Proudman's torment, which gave the Evil One such pleasure. He had hoped that Proudman's personal demons would have moved him into more self-destructive behavior, and made him more easily susceptible to Satan's temptations; drugs, alcohol, depression...even suicide. But Proudman had found Christ and realized salvation. Now all Abaddon could do was perpetuate the images of the past in Geoffrey's nightmares, and enjoy a small measure of devilish satisfaction in the residual pain still in Proudman's subconscious mind.

Geoffrey tried to close his eyes and go back to sleep. But the faces were unrelenting. It was 3:30 in the morning and the camp was quiet now. He reached for his flute and adjusted the bird over the tone hole so that he could play quietly, but retain the quality of the notes. He began to play and to improvise, letting the Spirit move him and his music. A sense of peace and calm overtook him, and the faces of the dead retreated to the recesses of his brain, where they seemed to lurk, waiting for the opportunity to come screaming out of the darkness, when next Proudman's head touched a pillow.

Simon and Rachel lay in each other's arms in Rachel's tent. It was their first night together and the best they could do was to push two cots together and cover them with several blankets to cushion the ridge in the middle. The couple was tired, but content. The reception had been incredible, thanks to Moishe's over-the-top efforts. Best of all, they were finally husband and wife.

"Wow," Rachel sighed. "What an amazing night."

"Indeed," Simon agreed. "So, it's our wedding night and we're in a tent on a very lumpy bed. Nothing but the best for my wife, that's what I always say."

"Well, husband," Rachel smiled at the sound of her words, "technically it is the morning after our wedding night and the accommodations are not that bad, really."

"You're a good sport, wife." Simon grinned at his first opportunity to call her that.

"So, it's too late to try getting any sleep..." Simon kissed her neck playfully.

"I'm listening," Rachel responded, encouraging him to continue.

Simon rolled on top of Rachel, kissing her passionately, as the cots beneath them suddenly separated in the middle from the concentrated weight. The amorous duo hit the hard ground with a thud, knocking the wind out of Rachel, while knocking the romance out of the moment at the same time.

"Ouch," Rachel groaned. "That hurt."

Simon began to chuckle. Rachel soon joined him and the two interrupted lovers dissolved in laughter.

"Might as well just stay on the ground," Simon reasoned.

Rachel agreed. "Tell you what, husband. Tomorrow, let's respond to our invitation to check out the tomb at Hakeldama. We can go to Jerusalem tomorrow night and stay in a great hotel with a magnificent bed. Sound good?"

"Count me in, wife." Simon kissed her softly and closed his eyes. Rachel moved in closer and allowed herself to relax. Sleep took them both. Passion would wait a little longer.

Jessie sat on his bed at the monastery and stewed. He was in a dangerous spot and he knew it. But, it was far too late to turn back now; to attempt to do so would have deadly consequences. He tried to think of his mega-church, where thousands of people would come and receive his message and praise him for his good works. He would be glorious.

He looked at the clock and grumbled. It was nearly 4:00 in the morning. He couldn't sleep and he needed something to occupy his restless mind. Jessie decided to pay the captive girls a visit in the bowels of the monastery. Tormenting them might prove entertaining.

Missy and Olivia drifted in and out of broken sleep. The straw mats they slept on were scratchy and thin, providing little relief from the hard stone floor. Missy wished for a shower and some clean clothes. Olivia wished for something hot to eat. Stale, cold sandwiches were the only thing Jessie had been feeding them. As the girls stared at the stone ceiling, their hearts jumped as the familiar clanking of the keys in the outer door caught their attention. It wasn't time for breakfast already, although Missy wasn't entirely sure what time of day it was. It just seemed early by her internal clock. The girls sat up and looked toward the door in frightened anticipation.

Jessie pushed the door open and stepped inside carrying a bottle of cheap wine and a deck of cards. "Okay, girlies," he announced, "it's time to play cards and drink."

"And what if we don't want to play cards with you?" Missy said defiantly.

"I don't drink wine," Olivia objected.

"You'll play cards or I'll find something else for you to do that won't be nearly as pleasant," Jessie threatened.

"Okay, okay," Missy conceded.

"So, here's the game," Jessie slurred. "Blackjack. Loser drinks."

"And winner gets what?" Missy asked.

"Don't know, let me think..."

"How 'bout if we win we get a hot meal and a shower," Olivia suggested hopefully.

"Deal, but if I win, you lose a finger each," Jessie smiled demonically as he produced a pair of tin-snips from his back pocket.

The girls recoiled in horror. "Forget it! I'm not playing," Olivia stated emphatically.

"Then I'll just go ahead and cut off two fingers each for forfeiting," Jessie replied, moving in on Olivia while snapping the tin-snips together menacingly.

"No!" Missy interjected. "Stop! Okay, we'll play. Just don't touch her fingers..."

Jessie grinned and backed off of Olivia, sticking the snips into his back pocket. He turned the toilet bucket over in the corner, dumping its contents and then inverted it to use as a stool. Sitting heavily, he shuffled the cards on his meaty thigh. Eyeing the girls and enjoying their anxious faces, Jessie dealt each of them a card. He looked at his, carefully shielding it from view. His first card was a king of spades. His smile quickly reverted to a poker face.

"So, let's make sure we understand, Jessie. If either one of us beats you, we both win. Right?"

"Yep. So, dealer takes a card." Jessie dropped a queen of diamonds onto of his face-down king. "Dealer sticks. Do you want a card?"

Missy looked at her card. Her heart pounded as she found a queen of hearts. "I'll take one."

Olivia looked at her card and felt an icy panic shoot through her body. It was a three of clubs. Not good. "I'll take one too."

Jessie dealt Olivia a card. The nine of spades came to rest in front of her. She had twelve. "I'll take one more."

Jessie dealt her a third card. Olivia cringed. The jack of spades put her into the loser's column. She revealed her cards and began to cry, sitting on her hands in an effort to hide her fingers from Jessie's snips. Jessie pulled the snips from his back pocket and waved them in Olivia's face, laughing maniacally.

He then tossed Missy a second card. As the card spun on top of her first card, she saw the king of hearts come into focus as the card stopped spinning. She had twenty. She eyed Jessie, searching his eyes to see if twenty would be enough. A tie would result in the loss of a finger. She closed her eyes and prayed silently.

"God? I'm kinda new at this prayer thing, but I know enough to know that You are in control of all things. Please help me decide. Do I take another card or do I stick? In Jesus name. Amen"

Jessie grew impatient. Well, girlie? Card or no card? You've got ten showing. What'll it be? My snips and I are growing impatient."

Missy tried to calculate the odds of an ace being the next card. Conventional wisdom would dictate that she should stick on twenty. She looked up at the ceiling and turned the decision completely over to God. "This is not about chance," she told herself, "this is about God's divine hand in my life." She turned her bottom card over, revealing the other royal heart.

"I have twenty. Hit me."

Jessie looked at her in disbelief. "What kind of idiot takes a card with twenty showing? Those fingers are mine! You're gonna bust for sure!" He flipped Missy a third card. The ace of hearts came to rest on her stack.

"Twenty-one. I win...God wins. Jessie, God wins."

Jessie growled as he turned over his cards. "Dammit!" He swore as he kicked the foul smelling bucket across the cell. "I ought to take your fingers anyway," he yelled.

"A deal's a deal, Jessie. We keep our fingers and we get showers and a hot meal. Because, if we don't, Jessie...then the mighty God who just pulled a queen of hearts, a king of hearts and an ace of hearts out of your deck, is going to rain down on you with such vengeance, that you will regret the day you messed with two daughters of the King!"

Jessie raged inside, but relented out of fear. He had come to the realization that he suddenly believed there was a God. It hit him like an oppressive weight. He had never really believed it before, but his skeptical mind had finally connected the dots. Satan was real; Jessie knew it because he was serving him. So it stood to reason, then, that God was real too, and He was on the opposing team—the winning team. Jessie suddenly felt small and trapped. Hastily he left the girls alone, locking them in as he left.

Missy and Olivia grasped hands. They had won. God had given them the victory and hope was rekindled within them. They smiled at each other knowingly. What a satisfying feeling to overcome fear and intimidation through the power of the Living God. Showers and hot food were on their way, but more importantly, they knew that even in their dungeon, God was present and on their side. They were Daniel in the den of lions.

chapter

TWELVE

But the eleven disciples proceeded to Galilee, to the mountain which Jesus had designated.

When they saw Him, they worshiped Him; but some were doubtful.

And Jesus came up and spoke to them, saying, "All authority has been given to Me in heaven and on earth.

Go therefore and make disciples of all the nations, baptizing them in the name of the Father and the Son and the Holy Spirit,

teaching them to observe all that I commanded you; and lo, I am with you always, even to the end of the age."

- Matthew 28:16-20

It was early Sunday morning, and one by one, Geoffrey, Angelica, Jordan, Moishe, Simon and Rachel, drifted across the camp and into the mess tent in search of coffee. Mumbling good mornings to one another as they sat together at one of the round, linen-covered tables left over from last night's reception. Around them, the caterer's clean-up crew was already removing decorations, linens, lights and tables. The mess tent was beginning to return to its former drab, utilitarian state.

"I didn't expect to see you two newlyweds up so early this morning," Moishe addressed Simon and Rachel.

"We decided to get an early start," Rachel explained. "We're planning on going into Jerusalem today to a hotel. Then on Monday we are going to the monastery at Hakeldama to get a look at the tomb they think they have discovered."

"That sounds interesting," Jordan said fuzzily. "I'm in."

"I was hoping that you all would join me this morning at the *Radiant UMC* camp at Lower Herodium," Angelica offered. "They've invited the remnant of *The Gathering,* who are still here, to a final Sunday service this morning at ten o'clock. Then they are packing up and going home...I guess they finally got a flight out."

"You're not going with them, Angelica?" Simon asked.

"No," Angelica said, smiling at Geoffrey. "I've decided to stay with Geoffrey and return home with him." She kissed Geoffrey's cheek and rubbed his back with one hand while sipping her coffee with the other.

"Indeed." Simon grinned at the two of them.

"Anyway," Angelica continued, "I want to say goodbye to them and would love for you all to meet them before they go."

"I think it's totally appropriate to close this chapter of our discovery with a worship service," Geoffrey spoke in support of Angelica's suggestion.

"Let's do it," Simon agreed. "We can go to the service on our way to Jerusalem. Then Monday morning we can see what great discovery awaits us at Hakeldama. The team all back together again...almost, anyway...it will be a grand adventure!"

"But first," Moishe interjected, "let's see if the cooks have been busy this morning preparing breakfast."

The team settled in to a morning meal together before church. There was a sense of enthusiasm for assembling with the remaining seekers left over from *The Gathering*. And, there was excitement about meeting Angelica's friends; she had become one of the team and her friends were now significant to all of them as an extension of her. Also, there was a sense of exuberance, a sense of discovery, which occurs for archaeologists each time they embark on unearthing a new site. The thrill of seeing things long buried. The entire team moved with renewed energy as they finished breakfast, packed, and loaded into Moishe's Land Rover for the drive to Jerusalem, with a stop in Lower Herodium for the *Radiant* worship service. Already, the seekers were gathering around the pool at Lower Herodium, waiting for the service to begin.

As the team rolled into the *Radiant UMC* camp, Angelica waved at Matt and Michelle, who greeted the team. "Hey! We wondered if you would make it for the final service," Michelle hugged Angelica as she climbed down from the Land Rover.

"Wouldn't miss it," Angelica responded and hugged Matt.

Several of the *Radiant* missionaries, seeing that Angelica was back, hurried over to welcome her. Cris, Bre and Allie gathered around her excitedly, wanting details of her adventure. Angelica, hugged them all and introduced the team, "Everybody, this is Simon and Rachel Cross, newly wed yesterday! And this is Moishe Silbermann, a great friend. And this is Jordan Goldberg, archaeologist and friend. And you have already met The Reverend Geoffrey Proudman, priest and...my boyfriend!" Bre and Allie squealed in delight.

"Father Proudman, I know this is short notice, but we were essentially going to have a praise and worship service.

Would you be willing to give us a sermon?" Matt offered hopefully.

"Wow," Geoffrey responded. "I hadn't really expected to preach this morning. Don't know if there's a sermon in me...maybe just a homily?"

"That would work," Matt said thankfully. "So, we'll get started with the music and then I'll invite you up to preach for as long as the Spirit moves you. Work for you?"

"Let's do it!" Father Proudman said enthusiastically. The truth was, Proudman was always ready to preach. He loved sharing God's word with the people. It was priestly. He liked doing priestly things. He loved being God's instrument. It made him feel useful and fulfilled. The mass of people was 5,000 strong. A small remnant considering the millions that surrounded Mt. Herod at *The Gathering*. These were the faithful who were left waiting for transportation home or simply needed guidance as to what they should do next with the truth they had heard and the new direction in Christ they were on.

As Matt, Michelle and the music team finished their set, Matt motioned Geoffrey to take the platform. "We have a special treat for all of you this morning at our last Sunday service here in Israel. The Reverend Geoffrey Proudman, spiritual leader of the team who discovered the scrolls in the mikveh, is here to speak to you. Father Proudman..."

Proudman rose onto the platform and looked out over the crowd. He closed his eyes and prayed, as he often did before preaching, "Father, remove me from this equation. Use me as your voice. Let the people hear your words, not mine. In Jesus' name. *Amen.*"

He began to speak. "In the 28th Chapter of the *Book of Matthew*, after our Savior was risen from the dead, he met his eleven disciples (Judas had committed suicide) on a mountain in Galilee. As he spoke to them, he reassured them that he was, indeed, the Risen Christ. He asserted his God-given authority over creation; over heaven and earth; over all things and over all people. It was this authority, as the Exalted and Risen Lord, which gave weight to his command to the disciples to go and make disciples of the nations.

Jesus told them to make disciples of all people by doing three very specific things: He told them to *go*, to *baptize* and to *teach*. He told them to *go,* because *going* requires action, which results in momentum—a gradual building up of energy into an unstoppable force. He told them to *baptize,* because baptism is symbolic of transformation, of dying to sin, and of being reborn in the power of the Holy Spirit, making the baptized a new creation in Christ. And he told them to *teach,* because only through continued exposure to the Truth and proper observance of the Way, could the new disciples learn accountability to their Faith.

Jesus, with this command, launched the evangelical mission of the Christian church, beginning with his original eleven disciples, who made disciples, who made disciples, and so forth, over the vast expanse of years until the responsibility for disciple-making landed squarely on us, the present-day Christians. We are inheritors of a royal decree, a command issued by Christ himself, who did so by the authority granted him as a person of the Trinity. It is not by coincidence that Christ instructed us to baptize disciples *'in the name of the Father and the Son and the Holy Spirit...'*

And, Jesus did not place the future of the church in the hands of disciples, then or now, leaving us on our own to accomplish this important mission with out guidance, or by our own power. No! He promised us that he would be with us *'always, even to the end of the age.'* His presence, his power has remained and will always remain with us, giving us what we need to carry out the command.

Why is this relevant today? What does it mean to the church-going Christian, faithfully attending church on Sundays and Wednesday nights? What does it mean to the consistent member of the congregation, regularly sitting in the same pew week after week, warmly greeting fellow members of their community of faith in the comfort of their own church, Sunday after Sunday, pot-luck after pot-luck, week after week, and month after month? The answer might astonish you. It might astonish you because, if, in the days that fall between the Sundays and the Wednesdays, the church-goer is not *going, baptizing* or *teaching*, then they are stagnantly disregarding their duty as Christians. Their collective inactivity outside the walls of the church is the single biggest reason for the decline of the church in modern times. This may seem a bit harsh, but I say this to challenge each of you. I say this to make you aware, if you are not engaged in The Great Commission of our Lord and Savior, then you are part of the problem.

I want you to wake up and be a part of the solution! Get up, get going! Talk to people outside of your church about your Faith! Be an example to them with your life and the fruits of the Spirit that you demonstrate. Engage them. Invite them in to your church. Who cares if they end up sitting in your pew! Teach them so that eventually they can be teachers. It is your responsibility to not only know Christ, but to make him known!

In Paul's second letter to Timothy, he charges the soldiers of Christ to *'preach the word'* and to *'be ready in season and out of season'* to *'reprove, rebuke,* [and] *exhort, with great patience and instruction. For the time will come,'* he says, *'when they will not endure sound doctrine; but wanting to have their ears tickled, they will accumulate for themselves teachers in accordance to their own desires, and will turn away their ears from the truth and will turn aside to myths.'*

Paul warns us of the consequences of remaining huddled together behind the comfortable walls of our church, all the while letting the world receive its instruction from feel-good teachers, who merely say what makes the people feel good; true or otherwise. Paul tells us to *'be sober in all things, endure hardship, do the work of an evangelist, fulfill* [our] *ministry.'* In this way we secure souls for Christ and rescue people from eternal separation from God. There is nothing more important. As Christians it is our mission, and the proper response to Christ's command."

Proudman turned and quietly left an empty platform. There was not so much as a cough from the multitude. The Holy Spirit had descended on Lower Herodium and every person gathered there felt renewed in their purpose. The people began to disperse, talking softly and reverently about the spiritual experience they had just shared. If they had not fully understood their role as Christians before, they had total clarity now. They could not wait to put the Great Commission into practice when they finally made it back home.

The team gathered around Geoffrey and embraced him in a group hug. They exchanged farewells to the *Radiant* mission team and boarded the Land Rover for Jerusalem. "That was inspired," Angelica said to Geoffrey as the Land Rover bounced toward the road.

"Thank you, sweetness. But it was all God."

"Yes, I know," she smiled at him, "but, I'm still proud of you."

Geoffrey kissed Angelica gently on her forehead. "Thanks, Babe."

chapter

THIRTEEN

And in the morning, 'There will be a storm today, for the sky is red and threatening.' Do you know how to discern the appearance of the sky, but cannot discern the signs of the times?

- Matthew 16:3

Moishe rolled up King David Street to The David Citadel Hotel and pulled up to the valet. The group disembarked from the Land Rover while porters unloaded their bags from the roof rack.

"Nice," Angelica said as she surveyed the hotel's glass-domed lobby.

"Wait until you see the view from your suite," Moishe said softly to her. "It has a view of the Old City that will take your breath away."

Angelica smiled at Moishe. "Can't wait!"

Simon, with Rachel clinging affectionately to his arm, checked in at the desk. "Reservation for Dr. and Mrs. Simon Cross," Simon told the clerk.

"Yes, Dr. Cross. Congratulations to you both! Here you are, the Presidential Suite."

"Presidential Suite? There must be some confusion. Just a junior suite will do."

"No confusion Dr. Cross. The room is already paid in full. Enjoy your stay, sir."

Simon looked at Rachel and shrugged. Rachel looked at Moishe, who winked at her. "Moishe, what did you do?"

"What? An old friend can't treat his two favorite newlyweds to a magnificent night at the David? Go on you two... enjoy! Life is short. You've been married for a day already... go...be alone. Take those marriage vows out for a spin and see what they can do!"

"Thank you my old friend. You really are the finest man on the planet." Simon hugged his friend appreciatively.

"This I know already!" Moishe responded. "Go!"

Geoffrey, with Angelica on his arm, Jordan and Moishe watched the couple disappear in the direction of the elevators. It gave them all great joy to see Simon and Rachel so happy.

"So," Moishe said. "You three all have your own suites waiting for you. My treat. I'd invite you back to my place for the night, but I'm afraid the place is crawling with workmen at the moment, sprucing the place up a bit after the Islamic Alliance's attack. I'm staying here too, so perhaps we should get cleaned up a bit and meet in the dining room for some lunch?"

"Moishe, you are a saint," Jordan offered.

"This, too, I know already!" Moishe laughed.

As Geoffrey, Angelica and Jordan headed off to their suites, Moishe stopped at the desk to speak to the concierge. "Please arrange for lunch to be delivered to Dr. and Mrs. Cross in the Presidential Suite immediately, and then please have dinner delivered at seven-thirty as well. Put it on the room, please. I'm covering their expenses. Oh, and a bottle of your best champagne with a bowl full of strawberries. Make that happen for me please?"

"Of course, Mr. Silbermann. It will be my pleasure."

"Good man!"

A half hour later, the team, minus Simon and Rachel, met in the dining room for lunch. "You were right, Moishe. The view from my suite is magnificent!" Angelica sat next to Geoffrey and across from Moishe as she spoke. "I have a private terrace and I can see the Old City perfectly!"

"I told you, dear one. Nothing but the best for my friends."

"You do spoil us, my friend. How can we ever repay you?" Geoffrey asked.

"Repay me? That's easy, my priestly friend. You say grace for us and then share a great lunch with me, giving me the pleasure of your company."

"I can do that." Geoffrey held out his hands and the rest followed suit, joining hands and bowing their heads as Geoffrey prayed. "Father, bless this meal provided from your bounty. Bless our friendship and our love for one another. May it please you and glorify you. In the name of Jesus we pray. Amen."

"Well said, Padre." Moishe signaled for the waiter. "My good man, bring us today's special and a good wine to go with it. Thank you."

"Very good, sir." The waiter nodded politely and hurried off.

Geoffrey looked around the table at his companions. "Well, we know that we are paying the monastery a visit tomorrow. But, what shall we do with the rest of our afternoon and evening? I don't expect we will see the newlyweds until sometime tomorrow morning, so I propose we get a look at the city."

"I think I've seen it many times before. I'm going to just relax in my room and catch a football match if I can find one on the television," Jordan said.

"I must go check on my house and my bistro, so you will have to excuse me after lunch, I'm afraid," Moishe added.

Proudman looked at Angelica. "Looks like it's just you and me, Babe. You in?"

"Absolutely! All I've seen of Israel is Herodium. Count me in!"

The foursome shared lunch and a couple of bottles of excellent wine. Moishe gave them a light-hearted lecture on why the wines complemented the meal and were the perfect selections for such a repast. Their time together was carefree and happy. Good food. Good fellowship. While upstairs in their suite, the newly married couple explored their passion for one another, oblivious to the world around them. All seemed in perfect order in their world. But, as often is the case, the storms brewing over the horizon seldom announce their coming. They simply rush in when least expected and unleash their fury, suddenly and without warning. Such a storm was not far off. Ignorance, in this case, was indeed, bliss.

Abaddon was growing weary of wearing the Kamal suit. He found his human host's body constricting and limiting. He was also growing agitated at the slow pace of his revenge. Patience was not in his character. Instant gratification was more his style. He paced Kamal's office like a caged animal; grumbling and growling. The rage was building up within and he could barely stand it. He thought about going down into the catacombs and murdering the two Christian girls, just to release some anger, but then decided against the idea when he thought about how much pain it would bring the priest, Proudman, when he forced him to watch the innocent girls die a cruel and agonizing death. What great fun that would be!

Jessie, prone to poor timing, knocked on the office door. Abaddon responded to the interruption, "What do you want, sniveling wretch!?"

"Uh, I can come back later if this isn't a good time."

"Well, you're here now, aren't you, maggot! What is so important?"

"I, uh, just wanted to let you know that the archaeology people called and said that they would be here tomorrow to look at the...uh...tomb."

"At last!" Abaddon was beside himself with anticipation. "Excellent! Very soon I will give those pests the crushing they so desperately deserve, and then I will shed this mortal skin and rain hellfire down on the Holy City and the world! It will be glorious!"

"Uh, sounds like a good plan," Jessie said weakly. "So, can I go now? I'll leave you to your revenge planning and go tend to the girls."

"Leave me, maggot. And, take care that nothing happens to the girls until I say so."

"Yes, I know. I'm just going to give them some lunch and clean them up a bit."

"Yes. Go."

Jessie retreated. He was always relieved to depart from Abaddon unscathed. His life before all this was miserable. Now it was miserable and scary. Jessie was full of regret. Not even a mega-church seemed worth all of this; but he was too undisciplined and too afraid to try and extract himself from the situation. He was getting exactly what he deserved. He knew it. He plodded to the kitchen and had the cook dish up two hot bowls of what appeared to be stew. The food was not gourmet, by any means, but it was tasty and wholesome. He grabbed a loaf of fresh baked bread off of a cooling rack and placed it on a tray with the bowls. This he carried down the dimly lit stairs to the girls' cell, making sure that none of the staff or monks saw him.

Hearing the keys rattle in the door no longer caused the girls the same level of anxiety as it did earlier. The girls felt protected, even in their captivity, they knew that God was present. Jessie entered and the aroma of the hot stew wafted in with him. Missy and Olivia eyed the fresh bread and steaming bowls. Their mouths began to water and their stomachs rumbled in anticipation of the good food that was coming.

"Here. Don't ever say that I welched on a bet." Jessie set the tray in the middle of the cell within reach of both captives. He turned to leave.

As he pulled the door behind him, Missy spoke out bravely, "You should let us go, Jessie. Whatever reason you brought us here, it's not worth it; you should just let us go. It's not too late for you to do the right thing. Just let us go."

Jessie didn't turn to face them. He simply muttered, "It's too late for that. It's not up to me. It's too late for you... and it's too late for me." He shut the door and locked it behind him.

Hungrily, Missy and Olivia devoured the spoils of their victory. They were giddy at the savory flavors and the saltiness; such a sharp contrast to the bland food on which they had been subsisting. Their appetites craved sustenance; they ate with abandon. Their bodies would need the nourishment to survive what was coming. The girls had no idea that Jessie was the very least of their worries.

Geoffrey and Angelica set out from the hotel on foot. This was the first opportunity that either of them had realized to see Jerusalem. They decided to walk past the Jaffa Gate, down Hativat Yerushalayim to the Ben Hinnom Promenade. The valley looked remarkably green and lush; not at all what Angelica expected. Life was returning to normal in the aftermath of the Islamic invasion. Families were picnicking on the grass and under the shade trees; children were playing soccer; everywhere people were enjoying their Sunday afternoon.

"So, in the morning we will go to St. Onuphrius Monastery and see if there is anything there," Geoffrey said to Angelica as the couple strolled the promenade hand in hand. "Then we need to think about getting a plane stateside."

"Then what?" Angelica asked tentatively. She really didn't want this adventure to end, but she too had responsibilities at home.

"Well, I've been thinking that maybe I would try and find a parish in Houston that could use a priest. That way, I could be closer to you and Freddie while we work on building our relationship. What are your thoughts?"

"I'd like that. I'd like you and Freddie to get to know each other too. It means a lot that you're willing to leave Austin and move closer to us. Thank you."

"It's what I want to do. What's more, I believe it is what God wants me to do."

"Well then, that settles it."

"Good."

"Very good," Angelica wrapped around his arm and put her head on Geoffrey's shoulder as they walked. The sun on her face was warm; and her heart was even warmer. She was falling in love and not resisting in the least, which was unprecedented in her experience. Geoffrey was already there, but reserved his emotions and passion so as not to cause Angelica any undue pressure. He was content to let her set the pace, despite the fact that he would willingly run at mach 3 if she showed any signs of being complicit. It was not just that he loved her completely, but more than that, he knew that their relationship was divinely orchestrated. She was the one. Of that there was no doubt.

Missy and Olivia dozed on their straw mats; the rich food having made them sleepy. Missy, by now sensitive to the slightest change in environment, thought she heard the familiar hum of the electricity, powering the single bulb hanging from the ceiling of their cell, change frequency; and when she opened her eyes it appeared less intense. It did not alarm her, but it was curious simply because it had never happened before. She listened for anything else that was different. She wished she had even the slightest clue of the time of day; or even what day it was. The cell insulated them, not just from the outside world, but from time...from the cycles of the moon and the sun. They existed meal to meal, with nothing but prayer and small talk to occupy the time between Jessie's tormenting visits. And, his visits were becoming increasingly unpredictable and threatening.

As Missy listened, she could hear Olivia's rhythmic breathing, occasionally interrupted by troublesome whimpers as she lived their nightmarish ordeal even in her sleep. Missy could also hear her own heart beating in her chest and the rustling of the mat underneath her head. As she took in these identifiable sounds in the quiet cell, she thought she heard something out of place; something unidentifiable. She couldn't quite place the sound, but it resembled a low rumbling at first. Missy tried to ignore the familiar sounds and to focus on the rumble. As she did, she began to hear the sound's nuances and the hair on the back of her neck prickled. She felt goose bumps rise on her arms and fear gripped her heart, causing it to pound in her chest rapidly. The rumble was, in fact, a low, guttural growl. No sooner had she realized what she was hearing, the volume increased and the solitary light bulb above flickered and went out.

"Olivia, wake up."

"What happened to the light? Now we are going to have to sit here in the dark until Jessie...Hey, is there a dog in here?"

"Do you hear growling, Olivia?"

"Yes, that's what I was talking about."

The light bulb flickered again and stayed on at one quarter its usual intensity, partially illuminating only the center of the cell, leaving the perimeter of the room in relative darkness. The girls moved quickly into the circle of light and peered into the dark edges. The growling continued from somewhere in the darkness.

"Where is that coming from," Olivia whispered fearfully.

Missy looked behind Olivia. Her eyes followed Olivia's leg chain from her ankle back toward the wall where it disappeared into the darkness. Missy wasn't at all certain, but it seemed to her that the darkness was even blacker at the end of the chain. Missy focused on that spot and stretched out, reaching for Olivia's hand.

"Give me your hand now, Olivia."

"Why?"

"No questions. Just do it now."

Just as Olivia stretched out and clasped hands with Missy, Olivia's leg chain began to pull steadily against her leg.

"Missy!" Olivia screamed. "Something is pulling my leg chain!"

The growling intensified as Missy gripped Olivia's hands tightly.

"Help me, Missy! Don't let it get me!"

Missy strained against the force pulling Olivia away from her. She could see eyes glowing in the darkness behind Olivia as she held on with everything she had. The growl became a vicious snarl and Missy could now clearly make out a dark form and saw a clawed, leathery hand reach into the circle of light and grasp Olivia by the ankle. The claws dug into Olivia's skin and she screamed, more out of horror than out of pain. Olivia rolled and kicked at the attacker with her free foot. The creature responded by raking a second clawed hand down Olivia's calf, tearing her flesh open as it did so. Olivia screamed again, more desperately. Missy, seeing the wound streaming blood onto the stone floor screamed equally as loudly.

The terror in Olivia's eyes was more than Missy could stand. She was losing her grip and she sensed that if she let go, the demonic creature would rip her friend to shreds. Missy did the only thing in her power. She prayed.

"Lord Jesus Christ, save us!"

As she said those words, the demon's growls and snarls turned into shrieks. Missy prayed again, "Lord Christ, save us!" Again the demon shrieked and loosened its grip on Olivia's leg.

"Keep praying!" Olivia screamed. "It doesn't like it!"

Missy spoke directly to the demon, "In the name of Jesus Christ, let her go!" The demon released its grip. "In the name of Christ, leave us alone!" The demon, obviously in distress now, squealed loudly in the corner. Missy was unrelenting, "Jesus Christ says leave!"

The demon shrieked, one last painful shriek, before it vanished into the blackness. The light bulb regained its full brightness and the two girls sat panting in the welcome light. Missy ripped a sleeve off of her shirt and gave it to Olivia. "Wrap your leg with this," she said. "Wrap it tightly. When Jessie brings us our next meal, we'll get you some help."

Olivia wrapped her leg and cried. "We're going to die, aren't we? What was that thing? Will there be more of them?"

"Well, if there are more of them, we know how to get rid of them now."

"I want to go home," Olivia sobbed. "I just want to go home."

"Me too," Missy responded. She could feel tears forming in her eyes. "Me too."

chapter

FOURTEEN

Those who seek my life lay snares for me; And those who seek to injure me have threatened destruction, And they devise treachery all day long.

- Psalm 38:12

Morning crept into Simon and Rachel's suite at The David Citadel Hotel like an unwelcome guest. The room was cool and the couple dozed in the softness of the king-sized bed. Rachel snuggled closely to Simon, drinking in the luxurious feel of newly-wedded bliss.

"Do we have to go see some dusty old tomb full of dusty old bones today?" Rachel pouted on Simon's chest, her eyes looking into his.

"Indeed we must, my love. It's all been arranged with the Archbishop. Remember?"

"Oh, bishop smishop," Rachel whined in a child-like voice.

"Indeed."

"Ok. But I'd rather stay here in bed with you...all day," Rachel kissed her way up Simon's neck in an attempt to get him to change his mind about vacating the comfort of their nest. Simon responded with a passionate kiss followed by a playful push toward the edge of the bed. "Really, Simon. Push me out of bed, will you?" Rachel grabbed a pillow and instigated an impromptu pillow fight.

Energy expended, Rachel wrapped herself in the top sheet on her way to the bathroom, where she drew a bath in the massive tub. "Well, if I have to go into a dusty old tomb, I want to start with a nice soak in a tub full of bubbles... and, there's room for company if you know anyone who is the least bit interested in joining me?"

Simon needed no additional prompting.

Geoffrey showered and dressed quickly, anticipating a day of discovery. He was excited about the possibility of discovering an archaeological treasure, to be sure, but he was more intrigued with discovering even more about Angelica. She was on his mind constantly. He had missed her the second he had kissed her goodnight and left her at her suite. He could hardly wait until he saw her again over breakfast.

Angelica's morning was more leisurely as she, too, soaked in a tub full of bubbles. How long had it been since she was in an actual bathtub, she wondered. She closed her eyes and thought about her entire experience in Israel. She thought about *The Gathering* and how amazing it was to witness all of the people receive Christ all at once. She thought of the miracle of the spontaneous rain that fell, and how Geoffrey had used the opportunity to baptize all of the people at the same time. She thought of the *Radiant* missionaries, holding worship services for the multitude, day after day and week after week, at the base of Mt. Herod. And, she thought about the time she had spent with Geoffrey, and how she was falling deeply in love with him. As she relaxed in the hot bath, the morning light streaming into her suite, she thought there was no more perfect world this side of heaven.

Moishe and Jordan met in the dining room and sat over their cups of coffee, letting the steam and the aroma exorcise the last remnants of sleepiness from their heads.

"I wonder what's keeping them." Jordan looked at his watch, noting that it was thirty minutes past the agreed meeting time.

Moishe chuckled. Jordan blushed and returned his attention to his coffee. Geoffrey entered the dining room and ordered coffee from a waiter on his way to the table. No sooner had he joined Moishe and Jordan, the waiter was filling his cup.

"So where is the lovely Angelica this morning?" Moishe asked with a raised eyebrow and a taunting tone in his voice.

"Well," Geoffrey avoided the bait, "when I last saw her, last night, she was entering her suite following an amazing goodnight kiss from yours truly. I suspect that she will be along any minute."

Geoffrey's timing was perfect as Angelica entered the dining room. Her mere appearance at the entrance caused conversations to stop and heads to turn. She was simply stunning. Geoffrey watched her all the way to their table, rising from his seat as she approached, kissing her cheek affectionately and holding her chair as she sat. Geoffrey signaled the waiter to pour her coffee. He enjoyed taking care of her every need.

By the time Simon and Rachel joined them, the others were on their second cup of coffee. "Sorry we're late," Simon offered.

"I'm not," Rachel countered. "It was a lovely morning."

"Indeed," Simon agreed.

The group enjoyed breakfast as Simon mapped out the plan for the morning. They would drive to the monastery at Hakeldama and meet with Father Superior Kamal Amman. He would lead them to the tomb and they would assess the find and determine how best to proceed if the find was worth anything. Perhaps it would mean bringing in ISAIAH and Ali's technical team. Perhaps not.

Geoffrey and Angelica would stay if the find panned out. If not, they would book the next flight back to Texas the following day. Jordan would either supervise the dig at Hakeldama, if there was one; or he would return to wrap up the dig at Herodium for Dr. Cross.

Depending on the magnitude of the find at Hakeldama, Simon and Rachel would either leave for a honeymoon in Paris next week, or immediately. Rachel hoped it would be immediately. Simon figured they could honeymoon in their suite at The David Citadel just as easily, so leaving next week for Paris didn't hold the same appeal for him.

The group finished breakfast and waited in front of the hotel for the valet to bring Moishe's Land Rover around. There was a freshness in the air; a newness and a sense of adventure. They could only imagine what treasures awaited them in the depths of the old monastery. Very soon the freshness would be replaced with the stench of a millennium's worth of hatred and evil; the newness would shrivel and die; the sense of adventure would become a reality of unbridled terror; and the only treasure they would unearth would be the ancient artifacts of death and destruction.

Jessie was tiring of his duties as keeper of the captive teenagers. He trudged down the stone stairs to the catacombs, carrying their breakfast, and unlocked the cell door, as he had done many times since their arrival at Hakeldama. He had stopped thinking about his promised reward... his mega-church. Nothing was worth this drudgery.

Jessie entered as he had always done, but he was caught off guard by the blood-stained floor and Olivia's crudely bandaged leg. Olivia was losing blood slowly and steadily; she was weak and lethargic. "What in the hell happened to her?" Jessie asked bewildered by the inexplicable carnage.

"Hell is exactly what happened to her, you jerk. One of your demonic friends attacked her," Missy said angrily. "She needs a doctor. Right now!"

"Not possible," Jessie responded. "Besides if she dies, it's probably the best thing for her anyway. Easier on her, ya know?"

Missy shuddered at the thought of bleeding to death being the "easy" way out. "You're just going to let her die,

Jessie? You brought her all the way here by airplane so she could bleed to death in this cell? That's just stupid."

Jessie thought for a moment. His instructions were to make sure nothing happened to them. Abaddon had made that crystal clear. If the girl died on his watch, he would have to face Abaddon. "Alright," he conceded, "I'll get her some help." As Jessie stepped toward the cell door to leave, Abaddon entered, blocking his path. Fear washed over Jessie. Even in his guise as Kamal, Abaddon had an oppressively sinister aura about him.

"What is this? What have you done to the girl, maggot?" Abaddon's displeasure surfaced rapidly. He grasped Jessie by the neck with one hand and lifted the 350 pound man off the ground as if he were lifting a small child. "I told you that nothing was to happen to them until I said so! Was this not clear to you, imbecile?"

"Yes," Jessie squeaked.

"He didn't do it," Missy couldn't believe she was defending Jessie. "It was some kind of demon-creature."

"Impossible! None would dare to go against my orders!"

"She needs a doctor. She's bleeding to death," Missy pleaded.

"We can't have that, can we?" Abaddon chuckled and set Jessie down on his feet. Jessie fell to the ground coughing.

"Who are you?" Missy asked cautiously. "You're dressed like a priest, but everything about you screams evil."

Unable to resist an opportunity to show off a bit, Abaddon turned his attention to Missy. "You are wise beyond your years, child. Such a pity you are so...misguided...in your choice of savior. Your observation is correct. I am not a priest. I am so much more." Abaddon paused, as if he were completely captivated by his own self-admiration. "Would you like to see the real me, child?" Abaddon smiled sweetly.

"Um, probably not," Missy replied honestly. In truth she had no desire to see what kind of creature could lift Pastor Jessie off the ground with one hand.

"Well I will show you anyway." Abaddon hadn't the slightest interest in Missy's opinion or desire. He peeled off Kamal's body and discarded it, and stood, full of himself, before the girls. His pale white skin seemed overly taught, revealing lean muscle and blue veins. His black eyes penetrated Missy's frightened stare. His body was wet and glistening in the dim light. She felt fear, dread and intense loathing for the figure standing in front of her.

"I know who you are," Missy whispered breathlessly. "You're the devil...Satan." Merely acknowledging him made Missy extremely uncomfortable. She searched her mind for some defense against the ultimate evil confronting her. She was so new to her faith, but she trusted in her heart that it would protect her if she could only gather her thoughts enough to put it into practice.

Abaddon circled the girls. Olivia's weakened state was causing her to fade in and out. Everything transpiring around her seemed dream-like. Her eyes followed Abaddon as he circled them. She moaned helplessly.

"Yes, I am Satan. I am known by many names, but I like that one best of all, don't you? It conjures up all sorts of imagery in your delicate little head, doesn't it, child? Makes you frightened and awe struck, I suppose?" Abaddon knelt down in front of Missy and cupped her chin gently in his hand. Missy pulled away, reacting to the coldness of his touch. Abaddon grabbed her face tightly and pulled her face to his. "Before this day is over, child, you and your little friend here, and the rest of the Christ-lovers, will bow down before me and call me master."

"I don't think so," Missy said smartly. "You can kill me, but my soul belongs to Jesus. You can't touch that part of me...ever."

"We'll see, child," Abaddon gave her face a final squeeze, "We'll see." Then, turning to Olivia, he placed his hand on her tattered leg and closed his eyes. "We can't have you leaving for heaven so easily, little one. Stay a while and enjoy the show." The wounds on Olivia's leg closed and vanished as if absorbed into her body. Olivia stirred and opened her eyes. Satan looked back at her. Olivia was speechless, terror gripping her as Lucifer's soulless gaze prevented her from moving or uttering so much as a whimper.

Satan stood and retrieved his Kamal suit from the corner where he had tossed it. Smiling and satisfied he had made the desired impression, he stepped over Jessie as he left the cell. "Get up, maggot. We have work to do before the others arrive."

Jessie got to his feet and departed, intentionally avoiding eye contact with Abaddon or the girls. His shame was overwhelming. Abaddon hurried up the stairs, Kamal's body over his shoulder like a sport coat. Jessie trailed slowly, defeated. As Satan disappeared down a corridor, Jessie took another passage to the courtyard. There were tourists listening to a guide explain the history of the monastery and surrounding area. He walked past them disinterestedly to the groundskeeper's storage shed. Rummaging inside for a few minutes, he emerged with a length of rope and walked back across the courtyard the way he had come. The visitors continued to focus their attention on the guide, who was now telling them the history of Hakeldama and the story of Judas, who hung himself from a nearby tree out of shame for having betrayed Jesus. As the tourists listened intently, the tree behind them rustled, and a dull thud and crack caused them to disengage from the guide, and they turned and looked. Horror greeted their eyes, as Jessie swung at the end of a rope from one of the courtyard's larger trees. His feet twitched slightly and his eyes bulged. A woman screamed.

Abaddon, now back in his Kamal suit, rushed out into the courtyard to investigate the commotion. He eyed Jessie and smirked. "Ladies and gentlemen, please, follow your guide out of the courtyard. The authorities have been called and we will deal with this unfortunate situation." He ushered the visitors out, as some looked back at the scene in disbelief. "He was unstable," Abaddon reassured them, "but we never thought he would do this. Everything is under control, now. Please be careful as you exit. Thank you."

Once the tourists were gone, Abaddon returned to the hanging Jessie and stood below him. "Idiot. Who do you think you are? Judas? I will deal with you later in Hell. Right now, I have to let the authorities take you so that all will be in order when Dr. Cross and company arrive." Abaddon reached for Jessie's pant leg and gave his body a spin as he smiled and walked away. Jessie spun to a stop, as the rope wound up, and then spun the opposite direction as the rope unwound. Abaddon chuckled, "Looks as if Jessie reached the end of his rope." Abaddon's chuckle became outright laughter that echoed eerily through the stone-walled monastery.

Archbishop Charalampous accompanied by his driver arrived at St. Onuphrius in time to see the panic-stricken tourists in front of the monastery. "What on earth is going on here?" he commented to his driver. He exited the car and overheard various tourists discussing the poor man hanging in the courtyard.

Rushing to the courtyard, the Archbishop was horrified at the sight of the twirling Jessie dangling lifelessly from the tree. He rushed into the building and down the corridor, bursting into Father Superior Kamal Amman's office.

"Amman! What the devil is going on here? There is a man hanging in your courtyard and I demand to know what you are doing about it!"

"Well, Archbishop, I've just called the authorities and now I intend to have some breakfast while I wait for them to get here. Care to join me?"

"Have some breakfast!? Are you mad? There is a dead man hanging from a tree outside!"

"Yes. And there is an Archbishop with a crushed skull in my office. Whatever shall I do?"

Abaddon grabbed the Archbishop's head in his hands and began to squeeze. The clergyman attempted a scream but to no avail. As his skull collapsed under the intense pressure of Abaddon's grip, Charalampous looked into Kamal's black eyes and knew that it was not Kamal.

"I'd give him a fifty-fifty chance that I'll see him again very soon," Abaddon said to himself. "It could go either way with that one." He grinned at his own dark humor.

chapter

FIFTEEN

Vindicate me, O LORD, for I have walked in my integrity,
And I have trusted in the LORD without wavering.

- Psalm 26:1

The Land Rover arrived at St. Onuphrius Monastery about the time that the coroner's wagon and police were rolling away. Father Kamal Amman, greeted the team at the front entrance enthusiastically. "Doctor Cross, it is a pleasure to finally meet you in person," Kamal said extending his hand.

Cross shook it and was taken somewhat aback by the coldness of Kamal's skin. "Father, Kamal, I am pleased to meet you as well. These are my colleagues, Dr. Rachel Cross, who also happens to be my beautiful wife, Dr. Jordan Goldberg, The Reverend Geoffrey Proudman, Miss Angelica Thorman and Mr. Moishe Silbermann."

"Welcome, all of you, to St. Onuphrius. It is not often we have such exciting and interesting visitors."

"It seems we aren't the only excitement today, are we Father Amman?" Geoffrey motioned toward the departing police cars.

"An unfortunate incident, I'm afraid. One of our staff took his own life, poor soul. We had no idea he was so... distraught."

"Indeed," Simon sensed Kamal was not as disturbed by the event as he should've been. But, then, perhaps it was just Kamal's way of dealing with the tragedy.

"So, perhaps I should lead you down to our little discovery. I know your time is valuable. I think you'll all find this very enlightening." Abaddon led the group into the monastery, through several corridors and down the stone steps to the catacombs. He smiled back at them as he placed the key into the lock of the cell door. "This is where we discovered something truly amazing," Abaddon said deceptively.

Cross and company were bristling with anticipation as the faux father superior opened the cell door. What could possibly be within? Was it the remains of one of the disciples? Would the discovery be one of the greatest finds since the scrolls? Cross peered into the dark room and fumbled for his flashlight as he stepped past Kamal into the room.

"Go ahead Doctor. You won't believe your eyes," Abaddon said temptingly.

Simon shined his light around the wall inside the room. He entered cautiously feeling for footing on the floor in front of him. The rest of the team followed him in; Geoffrey and Jordan adding their flashlight beams to Cross'. As they did so, Abaddon slammed and locked the cell door behind them cackling loudly as he did so. "Mine!" he shouted. "At long last you are all mine!"

The team spun around at the sound of the slammed door. "What is the meaning of this, Amman?" Cross shouted through the door. Abaddon continued to laugh.

Jordan felt the pull chain of a light switch brush his face. He pulled it and the room lit up. It was Angelica who saw the girls first. They were bound and gagged and in the corner of the cell. Their chains were gone, but they had been zip-tied, hands and feet, and their mouths had been covered with duct tape. "Geoffrey, look!"

Geoffrey rushed to the girls' aid and instantly recognized Missy. He un-taped her mouth carefully. Tears streamed down her face as she recognized Geoffrey. "Father Proudman, you came for us."

"I'm here, Missy. But, I'm afraid at the moment we are just as captive as are you. Let's get you both untied and you can tell us what in blazes is going on here."

"Well, I don't know exactly. All I know is we were leaving youth group one evening and we woke up here. We've been here a while. Pastor Jessie, from back home, kidnapped us, but that priest is not a priest at all!"

"What do you mean? Who is he?"

"Well, he can lift Pastor Jessie with only one hand. He can take off the priest, like he is just using his body, or whatever...and he is really Satan!" Missy looked at Geoffrey's eyes to see if he believed what she was telling him.

"Kamal is Satan?" Cross was confused. What makes you think that?"

"Ok. Like, he is really strong. And he wears the priest's body and he told us he was Satan. Did you not just hear me say that?" Missy was frustrated at their apparent inability to comprehend what she was telling them.

"Ok, Missy," Proudman comforted her. "We get it."

Geoffrey stood and huddled with Cross, Moishe and Jordan, assessing their predicament. Rachel and Angelica, worked on unbinding the girls and mothering them. Missy clung to Angelica, for the first time allowing herself to be the fearful, helpless child. Olivia sobbed in Rachel's arms, relieved that she could let her guard down for even just a moment.

Simon looked to Geoffrey, "So now what? How do we get out of here? Any of your former training ever get you out of a locked cell?"

"Not exactly. Especially not one with Satan on the other side of it. However, in order to deal with us, he will eventually have to open the door again. And, when he does, we can jump him."

"Jump him? Jump the Prince of Darkness?" Jordan interjected.

"I must concede, it sounds a bit...under thought," Geoffrey admitted. "Got any better suggestions?"

The other men shook their heads.

"Pray," Missy offered from Angelica's comforting arms. "We were attacked by a demon earlier. We prayed and it shrieked and vanished."

"Out of the mouths of babes," Moishe chuckled.

"Indeed." Cross nodded approval.

"Ok. When Satan opens the door to deal with us. We will jump him with prayer." Proudman offered his revised plan. "Only, I suggest that we don't wait until then to begin praying."

The others nodded in agreement. Angelica and Rachel helped Missy and Olivia to their feet. The group gathered in the center of the cell and clasped hands. Geoffrey bowed his head and began to pray in earnest for them to be delivered from Satan's grasp. "Father, we need you now. You see us in this darkness. Even the depths of this cell are not too deep for Your love and protection to penetrate. Hold at bay, the fear that binds our hearts and prevents us from clearly focusing on You. Send Your Holy Spirit into this cell and give us peace and strength to handle all adversity. Deliver us, Father, from evil. Protect us from the guiles of Satan and his demons. Bind Lucifer and cast him out of this place, back to Hell where he belongs. Save us from destruction, Lord. Keep us safe and in Your will. In the mighty name of Jesus we claim victory. Amen."

The group emerged from their prayer. "Look!" Moishe exclaimed. "The cell door is ajar."

Geoffrey opened it cautiously and scanned the outer passageway. It seemed clear. He walked quietly to the stairs leading up out of the dungeon and listened. It too seemed clear. He motioned for the others, who emerged from the cell cautiously. Simon moved next to Geoffrey, followed by Rachel, Angelica and the teenagers. Jordan and Moishe brought up the rear. Geoffrey put his finger to his lips, signaling for silence as they began their ascent up the stone steps. Upon reaching the upper corridor, Geoffrey peered carefully around the corner. Empty.

The group made its way to the main entrance of the monastery, seeing not a living soul as they went. Evening had fallen and the grounds outside the monastery were dark. The group moved cautiously to Moishe's Land Rover, still parked in front. Moishe got in and started the engine. "Come on!" he said to the others. "Get in!"

Geoffrey took the passenger seat up front. The two girls and Angelica crawled over the middle seat to the jump seats in the rear. Jordan, Rachel and Simon took the middle seat. Moishe pulled onto the road leading into the Hinnom Valley and sped away from St. Onuphrius. Missy and Olivia peered out the back, trying to see through the dusty window if anyone might be pursuing them. There was no one.

"That was easy," Moishe remarked.

"Too easy," Geoffrey offered.

"My thoughts exactly," Simon agreed.

The Land Rover rounded a bend as they descended into the valley. The night seemed much blacker than Moishe had ever seen. The headlights barely pierced through it to illuminate the road in front of them.

"Something's not right," Moishe said. "The headlights are just being swallowed up in the night. I can't see a thing."

"Try the high beams," Geoffrey suggested.

"These are the high beams," Moishe countered.

"Not good," Geoffrey conceded. "Stop, before we run off the road."

Moishe stopped. The blackness around them was oppressive. "Why are we stopping?" Olivia began crying. "They're going to catch us if we stop."

Rachel reached back and held Olivia's hand. "We're ok."

Moishe and Geoffrey disembarked. Simon and Jordan did likewise. The air around them was thick. There was a density to it and it smelled of kerosene.

"Why is the air so thick?" Jordan wondered out loud.

"Do you smell that? It smells like petrol and sulfur," Simon noted.

"Not sure what to make of it," Geoffrey added, "but I don't like it."

"As I see it," Moishe reasoned, "we should be somewhere above the Ben Hinnom Promenade. If we are careful, we can park the Land Rover and make our way down the hill to the Promenade below. Then we can follow it out of the valley into the city."

"But shouldn't we be able to see the lights of the city from here? And the Promenade should be lit as well. Where have the lights gone? Is there a power failure?" Jordan's nerves were showing through, despite his best efforts to remain calm.

There were no ready answers to Jordan's questions. Moishe parked the Land Rover on the narrow shoulder and the girls exited the vehicle nervously. The darkness was thick around them as the team descended, each one holding onto the person in front of them, as they negotiated the steep hillside; feeling their way one cautious step at a time. Even with flashlights, the way was dark and treacherous, as the lights barely illuminated the path just a few steps ahead.

After about an hour of tedious descent, the team ended up on the grassy, gently rolling terrain of the valley floor. Moishe led and within minutes they reached the hard surface of the Promenade.

"We're at the Promenade," Moishe announced. "All we have to do is walk that direction and we should end up in the Old City." Moishe pointed his flashlight in the direction he intended to go and began walking into the darkness. The group made better time on the hard surface of the Promenade and they began to feel as if they were on their way to safety. As they walked, they began to notice small fires igniting on the hillside on either side of them. First one fire, then another and another, randomly spaced. In their eerie glow, it appeared as if the very hillsides were moving, as black shapes crawled over their steep, rugged terrain with ease.

"I'm not liking this at all," Simon vocalized what everyone was feeling.

The figures surrounded them on all sides, slithering, they crept closer to the helpless group. Geoffrey kicked at a snarling demon as it got uncomfortably close. It spat at him and hissed. The demons grew even more aggressive and moved in on the team in force. Geoffrey and Simon punched and kicked until they were overcome by the relentless numbers of attackers. Moishe and Jordan suffered a similar fate and were pinned into submission by the host of demons. All the men could do was watch helplessly as the women and girls were dragged away screaming by the throng of demons.

For long minutes the demons tormented the men, scratching and biting them as they held them in place. Then, as suddenly as it had begun, the demons' attack ended. The demons backed off of the men who jumped to their feet and formed a circle facing outward, ready to try and fend off a second attack. The demons kept their distance.

The valley suddenly became illuminated and the men turned in the direction of the light. A huge burning altar at the end of the valley illuminated the area. Simon, Geoffrey, Moishe and Jordan could clearly see the demons on the hillside and all along the valley. They no longer paid any attention to the men in their midst, except to snarl and hiss at them and prevent them from leaving the valley floor.

"What...in the name of all that is Holy, what is that?" Moishe asked.

"*Topheth*," Simon responded. "The burning altar on which the children of Israel were sacrificed to Molech. Satan has reconstructed it."

"That's bad news," Geoffrey commented.

"Indeed."

The men advanced toward the altar. As they drew closer, they could see Rachel, Angelica, Missy and Olivia had been bound and hung suspended from huge wooden arms that could be pivoted into the burning altar where they would be consumed by the flames. Satan stood behind and above the altar looking down the valley at the legion of demons assembled there to witness the fulfillment of his revenge. Jessie's body sat limply in a wooden throne next to Satan. He was dressed in ornate robes and wore a pointed bishop's hat. Baal stood at the base of the fiery altar, ready to give the command that would send each of the girls into the fire.

Satan spoke to the men, "How do you like my *gathering*!" He laughed loudly. The demon throng followed suit. "And look!" Satan gestured to Jessie, "I promised this maggot a mega-church, and so he presides over this congregation of the fallen legion. I always keep my promises!" He laughed even more heartily.

Geoffrey spoke up, "What is it you want, Lucifer? Let these women go. They are daughters of Christ and you have no power over them."

"That's where you are wrong, priest. I have complete control over when they go into the fiery altar as a sacrifice to me. I simply wave my hand and my servant, Baal, will have them swung into the fire to roast like a pig on a spit."

"And what will you gain by that, Satan? You will merely send them to heaven and reward them for all time for their faithful service to God."

"You have no idea what they will do when faced with burning to death, priest. Here is my offer to you ladies: denounce Christ and your God and swear allegiance to me, and I will have Baal release you so that you will avoid the fire and live. Who wants to live tonight, hmmmm?"

Angelica summoned her courage and answered, "*Be gone, Satan! For it is written, 'You shall worship the Lord your God, and serve Him only.'*"

"Foolish choice, child. You will change your mind when the flames start licking at your precious flesh. What about you three? Do you want to burn or do you want to live? If you think that your God will keep you out of the fire, then go ahead and call out to him. Surely he will keep you from burning. *For it is written, 'He will command His angels concerning you to guard you,' and, 'On their hands they will bear you up, So that you will not strike your foot against a stone.'*"

Missy looked up at Satan and defiantly gave the same response that Jesus gave to Satan when tempted in the wilderness: *"It is said, 'You shall not put the Lord your God to the test.'"*

"We'll see if that theory holds up under fire, my foolish child! Last chance for you two," Satan directed his attention to Rachel and Olivia. "Live or die? Your choice."

Rachel looked into Satan's face defiantly, while Olivia, tears streaming down her face, simply looked away from the face of evil.

"Disappointing," Satan said. "Very well. As a reward for your faithfulness, you can watch the men die first. SEIZE THEM!"

At once, the demons rushed in on Simon, Geoffrey, Moishe and Jordan. They picked them up and carried them forward toward the altar. The heat was intense as they carried them past the wooden arms on which the girls were suspended. Moishe and Jordan struggled against the demons' hold, but no amount of resistance could possible overpower them. Geoffrey closed his eyes and looked for the face of God. Peace came over him and he began to recite from the depths of his memory, the 91st Psalm.

"He who dwells in the shelter of the Most High
Will abide in the shadow of the Almighty.

I will say to the LORD, 'My refuge and my fortress,
My God, in whom I trust!'

For it is He who delivers you from the snare of the trapper
And from the deadly pestilence.

He will cover you with His pinions,
And under His wings you may seek refuge,
His faithfulness is a shield and bulwark."

Proudman felt the demons holding him falter beneath him as they carried him. He felt the power of the Holy Spirit fill him and he resumed the Psalm with authority.

"You will not be afraid of the terror by night,
Or of the arrow that flies by day;

Of the pestilence that stalks in darkness,
Or of the destruction that lays waste at noon.

A thousand may fall at your side
And ten thousand at your right hand,
But it shall not approach you.

You will only look on with your eyes
And see the recompense of the wicked.

For you have made the LORD, my refuge,
Even the Most High, your dwelling place.

No evil will befall you,
Nor will any plague come near your tent."

The priest felt the demonic grip loosen even more. Several of the demons let go of him entirely and backed away from him in fear. Proudman felt energized by the Spirit.

"For He will give His angels charge concerning you,
To guard you in all your ways.

They will bear you up in their hands,
That you do not strike your foot against a stone.

You will tread upon the lion and cobra,
The young lion and the serpent you will trample down.

'Because he has loved Me, therefore I will deliver him;
I will set him securely on high, because he has known My
name.

'He will call upon Me, and I will answer him;
I will be with him in trouble;
I will rescue him and honor him.

'With a long life I will satisfy him
And let him see My salvation.'"

As Geoffrey's recitation came to a mighty crescendo, the demons dropped the men to the ground and wailed, covering their ears and cowering.

Satan angrily dressed down his demonic legion, "What are you wailing for, you sniveling cowards? These are merely spells and incantations designed to confuse you! They have no power. They are just words! Now cast them into the fire! Move you wretches!"

The demons regrouped and attacked again, carrying the men to the lip of the altar and tossed them into the flames one by one. Rachel screamed as her beloved Simon disappeared in the fire. Angelica watched, powerless as her future with Geoffrey went up in flames. Moishe and Jordan met the same fate, as the girls looked on in horror.

Satan roared in laughter, rejoicing in the accomplishment of his revenge. "Oh, this is so sweet. The taste of this revenge is like a fine wine on my palette. Baal, at your discretion, let's roast some tender girls, shall we?"

Baal signaled for the women to be pivoted into the center of the altar's fury. The demons laid into the crossbars at the base of the enormous wooden arms and they began to move the girls toward their infernal death. As the demons shrieked and hollered in their blood-thirsty frenzy, they one by one grew suddenly silent until there was no more revelry coming from the legion. The demons turning the wooden arms stopped and looked into the fire in amazement. Baal, confused at the silence stared in the direction of the altar to see what everyone was focused on so intently.

In the midst of the fire, the demons could see, not only the four men they had just cast into the fire, but also a fifth man walking around with them.

Satan called to Baal, "Was it not four men that we cast into the fire?"

"Yes it was, my lord."

"So why then are there five men walking about in the fire as if nothing is wrong?"

"I do not know, my lord."

Perplexed, Satan descended closer to the altar to get a better look at the inexplicable events taking place within the altar's raging inferno. As he peered into the flames, Simon, Geoffrey, Moishe and Jordan emerged. They were unharmed, their hair was not the least bit singed, their clothing was not scorched, and they did not have so much as the smell of smoke on them.

"This is not possible," Satan could not fathom this unexpected outcome. "Where is the fifth man that was in there with you?"

Geoffrey spoke with authority, "He is here, Satan. He is all around you. He is the Prince of Peace, Mighty God,

Our Deliverer. He has delivered us from your trap and from the fires of hell, both here in the Hinnom Valley and in the eternal abyss. You have no hold on us, Deceiver. You have no power over our souls or over our bodies. Release the girls and return to Hell. Go back into your hole or suffer the wrath of Almighty God."

The priest reached into his shirt and pulled out his crucifix. It was red hot from the furnace, and yet he could hold it in his hand without injury. He grinned into the devil's face and pressed the hot cross into Satan's pale white forehead, branding him with the image of Christ on the cross. Satan shrieked and recoiled from the intensity of the imprint.

"By the power of Christ, I command you to return to Hell. Be gone, Satan and leave this place in peace. Get thee behind me, Satan!"

Satan was speechless and powerless to act. In the face of incredible faith, he was nothing. There would be no counter attack today. Baal and the demons scattered into the caves and tombs on the hillside, using them as portals back to the safety of the abyss. Satan closed his eyes and fell backward into the fiery altar, choosing a hellish retreat over the wrath of God.

The altar vanished into smoke. The oppressive darkness of the demonic night subsided and the moon and stars shown brightly in the sky. A cool breeze flowed across the men and they smiled. Rachel, Angelica and the two teenagers found themselves unbound and on the grassy valley floor; gone were the huge wooden arms that had held them.

Simon rushed to Rachel and picked her up, holding her close. Geoffrey extended a hand to Angelica and pulled her up and to him. Angelica kissed his cheek. "You are a mighty warrior for God," she told him, "and I am so proud of you."

"Thanks, Babe. But it was all God."

"I know, but I'm still proud of you."

Moishe looked around and got his bearings; then he and Jordan headed off to retrieve the Land Rover, while the rest of the group sat in the cool grass to wait for them. Missy cuddled close to Angelica and held Geoffrey's hand. Olivia clung to Simon and Rachel. Their horrific ordeal was finally over.

"I need a shower and some Taco Bell," Missy announced.

"Indeed," Simon chuckled.

EPILOGUE

Therefore, since we have so great a cloud of witnesses surrounding us, let us also lay aside every encumbrance and the sin which so easily entangles us, and let us run with endurance the race that is set before us,

fixing our eyes on Jesus, the author and perfecter of faith, who for the joy set before Him endured the cross, despising the shame, and has sat down at the right hand of the throne of God.

For consider Him who has endured such hostility by sinners against Himself, so that you will not grow weary and lose heart.

- Hebrews 12:1-3

Geoffrey woke with a start and scanned the room. After a few tense, disoriented moments, his brain recognized that he was in one of Moishe's guest rooms. A beam of daylight streamed through a crack in the blinds and bounced off of his crucifix into his eyes. He squinted. Grasping the crucifix, he held it up and marveled at the fact that its imprint was now branded into Satan's forehead. The memory of last night's horror seemed surreal and rather like the memories one has after an intense motion picture.

Proudman kicked off the covers and sat up on the side of the bed, searching for a clock. He found one on a writing desk across the room and rubbed his eyes in an attempt to bring the digital numbers into focus. It was only 7:45 in the morning, but he was ready for coffee. More than anything, he wanted to see Angelica; just to be certain that his memory of her safety was indeed reality.

He pulled on his trousers and a shirt and padded downstairs to Moishe's kitchen. Moishe already had coffee brewed; and he, Simon and Jordan were at the breakfast table nursing their first cup. Geoffrey went directly to the coffee pot and filled the biggest mug he could find. He then joined the men at the table.

"Good morning, all," Geoffrey announced.

"That it is, Padre," Moishe said clapping Proudman on the back as he sat.

"I woke up this morning wondering if everything that transpired was real. I mean, if I didn't know better, I'd be inclined to believe that I dreamt it all."

"Indeed," Simon agreed. "I had to physically touch Rachel several times during the night just to reassure myself that she was safe."

"I know. I literally will not relax this morning until I see Angelica; just to know she's ok."

"I fully get that," Jordan added, "I poked my head into Missy and Olivia's room on the way down, just to satisfy myself that we had, in fact, rescued them. Olivia was on the phone with her parents, trying to explain to them where she's been all this time, and how she ended up in Israel. I'm sure they have been beside themselves with worry. Angelica went in and took over the phone call to reassure them that Olivia would be in good hands until we can get her on a plane."

"A terrible ordeal for all of us," Moishe commented. "But what an instrument of God you were, Padre. The 91st Psalm was brilliantly done. Such Holy power unleashed on that demonic scum! It was magnificent!"

"All glory to God," Geoffrey proclaimed.

"What was the purpose of kidnapping the teenagers, though? I don't get that part," Simon asked nobody in particular.

"I can only assume that Satan wanted to hurt me," Geoffrey offered. "Victoria, or Missy, was a student of mine after *The Gathering.* She is very special...a real young woman of faith, and I suppose Satan was trying to use her to inflict maximum revenge on me for my part in foiling his plan to conquer Jerusalem using Abbas and the Islamic Alliance. I suppose poor Olivia was just at the wrong place, at the wrong time."

Rachel entered the kitchen and Simon rose from the table to greet her. She kissed him gently and whispered a soft good morning into his ear. She then clung to him for several minutes; reassuring herself that all was well in the world again.

Angelica, Missy and Olivia entered the kitchen laughing and chattering. "We're hungry," Missy said, "What's for breakfast?"

Moishe rose from the table. "Not used to teenagers bouncing off the walls around here. This should be fun." He went to the refrigerator and began preparing the morning meal with a smile on his face. It was good to be back in his element, he thought.

Angelica moved behind Geoffrey's chair and draped herself around his neck. She kissed his cheek and hugged him for several minutes, grateful beyond words to be alive and close to the man she loved. Geoffrey felt peace come over him. Her safety meant all was in order. He felt blessed.

The events at Hakeldama and the Hinnom Valley were supernatural and largely unobserved by the average citizen in Jerusalem. For all intents and purposes, they suffered a prolonged power outage in the middle of the night, and they woke in the morning and went about their day none the wiser concerning Abaddon's night of terror. They had slept while the spiritual battle raged all around them.

Simon and Rachel departed Jerusalem for an extended honeymoon in Paris. Moishe arranged for a friend in Paris to lend them his summer home, and the archaeologists spent their time discovering nothing but each other for several weeks. Jordan Goldberg returned to Herodium to wrap up the dig for the University. He felt finally at peace with Miriam's tragic death, and it was good for him to be back at work. A little time each day is spent tending to Miriam's grave on the side of Mt. Herod.

The Reverend Geoffrey Proudman and Angelica returned stateside. They are engaged and planning a life together with Angelica's son, Freddie. They have also filed adoption proceedings for Missy, and her brothers, C.P. and Alex, and hope to unite as a family within the year. Proudman became head pastor at a non-denominational church near Angelica's home in Humble, Texas. His church's passion is to carry out The Great Commission of Our Lord and Savior Jesus Christ.

On his first Sunday to preach at his new church, the Reverend Geoffrey Proudman walked to the pulpit. He closed his eyes and prayed for God to use him as the instrument through which His words would flow. When Proudman opened his eyes, he paused to look out over the congregation; and he began to speak:

"There is a war raging outside these walls this morning. There is conflict between the powers and principalities of a dark and sinister world, trying desperately to win the souls of the unsaved. So, it is to the unsaved among us that I am specifically speaking. You should be aware, that the forces of evil will not necessarily appear to you as iconic images from a horror movie, but they will be nonetheless insidious and destructive.

These evil entities will attempt to infiltrate your life in the most seemingly benign ways. They may come to you in the form of peer pressure. They may present themselves as friends, telling you that everybody is doing it and that it's socially acceptable. They will prey on your weaknesses as human beings; on your predisposition to sin. They will entice you, and trick you, and deceive you using all manner of disguises. Their goal is to provide you with enough diversions and distractions to occupy your mind; to give you the illusion of happiness; to fill your heart with substitutes for real love and righteous satisfaction.

And if they can keep these distractions going long enough, through the course of your lives, so that you never open your hearts and your minds to the Truth, even at the moment of your death, then they win. The Truth. Understanding the Truth; that is the game changer for the unsaved. The Truth is this...are you ready to hear it? The Truth is simply this:

'For God so loved the world, that He gave His only begotten Son, that whoever believes in Him shall not perish, but have eternal life.' That's in the *Book of John,* third chapter, verse sixteen.

God gave His only son, Jesus Christ, as a sacrifice for our sins. Why was that necessary? Why did Jesus have to die for us? In *Romans,* chapter three, it tells us why:

'Since we've compiled this long and sorry record as sinners and proved that we are utterly incapable of living the glorious lives God wills for us, God did it for us. Out of sheer generosity he put us in right standing with himself. A pure gift. He got us out of the mess we're in and restored us to where he always wanted us to be. And he did it by means of Jesus Christ.

God sacrificed Jesus on the altar of the world to clear that world of sin. Having faith in him sets us in the clear. God decided on this course of action in full view of the public—to set the world in the clear with himself through the sacrifice of Jesus, finally taking care of the sins he had so patiently endured. This is not only clear, but it's now—this is current history! God sets things right. He also makes it possible for us to live in his rightness.'

So you know the *'what'* and you know the *'why'* about the Truth. Now you need to know the *'how.'* Let me start by saying that you cannot earn your way into the Grace of God. Nothing you can say or do will ever be righteous enough, will ever live up to the high, holy, standards God possesses. The only way for you to appear worthy in the sight of *perfect God* is to become *perfect man*; and on your own merit, you can never attain perfection. The only human being ever to walk this earth and live a life completely without sin is Jesus Christ. The only blood pure enough to be acceptable to God is the blood of Jesus. And therein rests our salvation.

Make no mistake about it...Jesus Christ is the only way to heaven. Jesus said, in *John* 14, verse six, '*I am the way, and the truth, and the life; no one comes to the Father but through Me.*' What a bold statement, isn't it? It is the kind of statement that bears some careful examination. As people with our souls in question, we ought not to pass this by without investigating who Jesus is and why he has the authority to make such a claim.

Upon careful examination, you will find that Jesus fulfills more than four hundred Old Testament prophesies dealing with the coming of, life, death and resurrection of the Messiah. The mathematical odds of one human being fulfilling all of those Old Testament prophesies are unfathomable. Even more remarkable, is Jesus' ability to cast out demons, and to heal the sick; demonstrating his rule over both the natural and the supernatural realms, by the authority of his oneness with God. Rest assured, Jesus Christ is the Messiah, and his authority is absolute.

So, then, back to the '*how.*' How do you accept the gift of Grace offered to you by a generous God through the blood of Jesus Christ? How do you go from unsaved to saved, from sinner to redeemed? Here's how. And this may seem profoundly un-profound to you because of its simplicity...nevertheless, this is the way to begin a right relationship with God through Christ according to *Romans* 10: 9-10:

> *'...that if you confess with your mouth Jesus as Lord, and believe in your heart that God raised Him from the dead, you will be saved; for with the heart a person believes, resulting in righteousness, and with the mouth he confesses, resulting in salvation.'*

Let me be clear; there is not a magical incantation that, by the mere recitation of which, you become saved. The recitation of the words is easy; the believing in the heart is a bit more difficult; it requires faith, trust and the courage to believe. And God sees the heart even more readily than He hears the words. Trust me on this. More importantly... trust God on this."

Geoffrey Proudman concluded his first sermon with a prayer and a blessing over his congregation. He simply prayed, "Father God, save those who need saving. Bless those who are already saved. In Jesus' name. Amen."

As he was about to call the worship team back up to play the closing song, he paused. The Holy Spirit was not done, and Father Proudman could feel the words forming in his thoughts. He then sat on the raised platform and looked at his beautiful Angelica sitting on the front row next to Freddie, C.P., Alex and Missy; he was filled with joy and he smiled warmly. When he spoke again, his words were softer and he spoke intimately to the hundreds of people quietly watching him.

"I have seen God reveal Himself to me through signs and miracles. I have seen God's hand vanquish armies with a mighty blow and, with that same hand, comfort a pair of scared teenage girls held captive at Satan's mercy. I have seen Him assemble a multitude, hungry for His Word, at the base of a remote mountain in a far off land, and I have felt His holy rain baptize millions all at once. I have walked in the midst of a fiery furnace and come away unscathed, with not so much as the smell of smoke on my clothing. I have seen Him strike down Satan, and Satan's demons, banishing them back to the abyss in the name of Jesus. And...I have been tormented by the faces of the dead, all my adult life, only to have them vanish in an instant at the acceptance of His Grace and Forgiveness.

But, even with all these things, I must confess to you today that the most impressive way God has moved in my life is through people like you, who embraced His Holy Word and then left the mountain top to carry His Word into the valley. So go. Leave the safety and sanctuary of your church, leave this mountain top experience and go spread the good news in the valley outside these walls. Go; carry out The Great Commission of Our Lord. Go make disciples of all the nations. All authority, in heaven and on earth, has been given to you through Jesus Christ. Go."

AFTERWORD

There is a compelling need in the world today for people of faith to step outside their comfort zones and to engage those who have not yet discovered God's grace and mercy. I cannot help but feel that there is an urgency to reach as many souls as possible before Christ's inevitable and imminent return.

While it is certainly true that no one knows the time of Christ's return, it is prudent for us to be ready for that joyous event now...*right now*. It is in that spirit that I wrote *The Mikveh Scrolls* and *The Yeshua Sanction*. It is my deepest desire that those in the community of faith would use these simple books as tools to engage seekers, those who need a relationship with the Lord, but who, for one reason or another are not inclined to immediately go right to the source of God's word: *The Bible*.

If my work inspires even one soul to delve deeper; to investigate the source material; to find the scriptures and truths contained within these pages and trace them back to their origin; then, I will consider the time and effort well worth the investment.

Christians, I implore you...honor the command issued to you by Jesus Christ. Spread the good news of God's grace through the death and resurrection of Christ; and take up the cross. Make disciples. Lead and teach. Make Christ known. There is no higher calling, and make no mistake, as a Christian you are, indeed, called.

A final thought for your consideration: In *The Bible*, the *Book of Hebrews* is the inspired word of God, written down by an unknown author. The third century theologian, Origen Adamantius, said, "Only God knows who wrote *Hebrews*." And perhaps, that is one of the things that make the wisdom contained therein so compelling. From its text, consider this:

Therefore, since we have so great a cloud of witnesses surrounding us, let us also lay aside every encumbrance and the sin which so easily entangles us, and let us run with endurance the race that is set before us, fixing our eyes on Jesus, the author and perfecter of faith, who for the joy set before Him endured the cross, despising the shame, and has sat down at the right hand of the throne of God.

For consider Him who has endured such hostility by sinners against Himself, so that you will not grow weary and lose heart.—Hebrews 12:1-3

What intrigues me about this scripture is the reference to the *"great cloud of witnesses surrounding us,"* which brings to mind that as Christians, we are watched. The unbelieving world analyzes our every action and reaction, for the purpose of critique or, much more preferable, emulation. If we are to make disciples of the seekers, then we must always remember to live out our faith and present to the world our Christ-like face. Granted, we will not be perfect. We will fall short. But the way we handle our failings and our shortcomings, in the public eye, is every bit as important, perhaps even more so, than our ability to stay between the lines of the narrow way.

I am further intrigued by the reference, *"...and let us run with endurance the race that is set before us, fixing our eyes on Jesus, the author and perfecter of faith..."* This is a compelling affirmation that there is indeed a sense of urgency to our mission as Christians. We are not called to *walk* through life. No! We are called to *run* like endurance runners, making disciples day-in and day-out. We are called to keep focused on the example set by Jesus, by keeping our eyes on him and remembering that he endured harsh treatment and death, even death on a cross, giving everything he had for the redemption of sinners like us. Can we as Christians give anything less?

Almighty and merciful God, in your goodness keep us, we pray, from all things that may hurt us, that we, being ready both in mind and body, may accomplish with free hearts those things which belong to your purpose; through Jesus Christ our Lord, who lives and reigns with you and the Holy Spirit, one God, now and for ever. Amen.—Book of Common Prayer

www.ingramcontent.com/pod-product-compliance
Lightning Source LLC
Chambersburg PA
CBHW022036240626
47154CB00007B/2437